AF226283

ON THE HUNT

A COZY QUILTS CLUB MYSTERY
BOOK 7

MARSHA DEFILIPPO

Copyright © 2025 by Marsha DeFilippo

All rights reserved.

This is a work of fiction. Unless otherwise indicated, all the names, characters, businesses, places, events and incidents in this book are either the product of the author's imagination or used in a fictitious manner. Any resemblance to actual persons, living or dead, or actual events is purely coincidental.

No part of this book may be reproduced in any form or by any electronic or mechanical means, including information storage and retrieval systems, without written permission from the author, except for the use of brief quotations in a book review.

For avoidance of doubt, Marsha DeFilippo reserves the rights, and publishers/platforms have no rights to, reproduce and/or otherwise use the Work in any manner for purposes of training artificial intelligence technologies to generate text, including without limitation, technologies that are capable of generating works in the same style or genre as the Work, unless publisher/platform obtains Marsha DeFilippo's specific and express permission to do so. Nor does publishers/platforms have the right to sublicense others to reproduce and/or otherwise use the Work in any manner for purposes of training artificial intelligence technologies to generate text without Marsha DeFilippo's specific and express permission.

To get the latest information on new releases, excerpts and more, be sure to sign up for Marsha's newsletter.

CONTENTS

PROLOGUE

The day was starting out perfectly. It was the break of dawn, with just enough daylight to walk through the thicket of trees without needing a flashlight. There'd been a light snowfall the night before, which meant it would be easier to track deer. Ted Hartley walked as quietly as possible, but the snow was crusty and his boots made quiet crunching noises. The air was crisp, but comfortable if you dressed properly, and he was an experienced hunter with the right gear. Little puffs of vapor clouds appeared when he exhaled.

Couldn't be a more perfect day, he thought as he looked up at the sky toward the tree stand suspended above him and the ladder he'd need to climb to get to it.

Must be at least twenty-five feet off the ground.

It was higher than others he'd used when he'd been deer hunting, but he wasn't afraid of heights.

Better get going before a buck spots you.

He slung the strap of his rifle around his shoulder and climbed up the rungs. As soon as he stepped on the stand, his stomach clenched and he sucked in his breath.

This doesn't feel right.

He heard an ominous creaking noise, and the stand tipped

sharply to the left. He windmilled his arms, trying to regain his balance, but the platform kept leaning. There was another loud crack, and it tilted into a vertical position and was hanging by only one bolt. His fingers clawed at the boards, but there was nothing for them to latch onto and he was falling to the ground, landing with a sickening thud and the world turned black.

The sound of footsteps crunching on snow was heard only by the squirrels and birds roosting in the trees. They watched as the human bent down and put his fingers on the man's neck, which was cocked at an odd angle.

"Worked out just like I planned it."

The figure rose and retraced his steps, walking leisurely backwards into the forest using a branch pulled off a pine tree to sweep away his footprints. The sun might melt them before Ted's body was found, but he wasn't taking any chances.

CHAPTER 1

Jennifer Ryder wrapped Rachel Hartley in a heartfelt hug. "It's so nice you see you again. I'm sorry it's under such sad circumstances, though." She released her embrace but held onto Rachel's arms and looked at her more closely.

She's lost weight and she's aged at least ten years, Jennifer thought upon seeing her sallow complexion, the dark circles below her eyes, and sunken cheekbones. Her clothes hung loosely from her tall frame. Jennifer's eyebrows scrunched together with concern. "How are you doing?"

"It's good to see you, too, Jen. In some ways, I can't believe it's been two months since Ted died, and at other times, it feels much longer. I still feel numb inside, but I know it will take time to heal." Rachel paused, pursing her lips to hold back her emotions before going on. "My first thought was to donate or dispose of Ted's clothes, but I couldn't bring myself to do it. When I heard about memory quilts, I knew you were the perfect person for this project. I thought of Eva because she lives right next door, but you did such a wonderful job coordinating the Project Linus donations for Summer Williams's celebration of life, I wanted you to do this."

A hit-and-run driver had struck and killed Summer Williams

in August. Jennifer had not only organized the quilt memorial for Summer; she and Eva Perkins and her other two Cozy Quilts Club friends had solved the case. That part, Rachel didn't know about, along with most of the other residents of Glen Lake.

"She would have done a fantastic job, as would any of our members. I'm honored to make a memory quilt for you, though. I've never made one before, but I've heard about them."

Rachel leaned over and pulled the laundry basket on the floor beside her chair in front of her. She stroked the shirt sitting on top of the pile and held it up to her nose, inhaling Ted's scent, forgetting for a moment that Jennifer was watching. *Are you sure you're ready to let them go?* her heart asked. Her emotions tugged at her, but at last her logical side answered *Yes, it's not forever.* She looked up and her eyes glistened, but she blinked to keep away the tears threatening to slide down her cheeks.

"I didn't know how much you would need, but I put in the shirts I knew I'd want to be part of the quilt." She slid the basket toward Jennifer.

"Do you know what size you'd like me to make or a pattern you'd like me to use?"

Rachel nodded her head. "I've been looking at different patterns online. There are so many beautiful ones to pick from, but when I saw the name Hunter's Star on one site, I knew that was the one. You might think that odd since Ted died in a hunting accident, but he so looked forward to deer season every year. Even in the years when he didn't get a deer, he'd always come home feeling less stressed. He said it was the connection with nature. If you have enough material to make a queen size, that would be my first choice. I'm not a quilter, though, so I have no idea if you need more."

"As it happens, I've got the Hunter's Star pattern on my list of quilts I want to make, and I already have the instructions. There are a lot of shirts here." Jennifer thumbed through the pile. "There must be at least a dozen. I'll need to buy some extra fabric for the backing and borders anyway, but if you don't mind if I mix in some new material for the blocks, too, it won't be a problem to make a queen size. I'll use as much as I can of Ted's clothes before adding the new stuff."

"No, I don't mind at all. I guessed that would be the case and I leave it to your discretion."

"Do you have a deadline for when you'd like this finished?"

"Not at all. I know you must have a hectic schedule with working part time at your insurance agency and a husband and two teenagers at home."

"They do keep me busy. This year is busier than usual with Matt's graduation coming up in May and sports for him and Nicky, but I should be able to fit this in with no problem. Dave is an easy person to work for and if I need more time off, he'll let me take it if it's slow at the office. That's one advantage of being married to your boss," Jennifer said, smiling.

"Going back to work has been both a blessing and a challenge. I love teaching and being around all that kid energy has been good for me. The hardest part has been getting myself there in the morning, but once I'm in my classroom, I'm good."

Jennifer nodded. "That makes a lot of sense." She rose to her feet, signaling Rachel she was ready to go.

"I'll get your coat. Do you need any help carrying out the basket?" Rachel asked.

"I keep some bags in my pocketbook in case I forget to take my reusable ones into the store when I'm shopping. It's not a problem for groceries, but after forgetting to take them when I'm in other stores more times than I can count, this was my solution. I think I can fit all of them in those so you can hang onto the basket." She pulled the totes out of her purse and began filling them with the clothes. "Ted wasn't afraid of colors, was he? These are going to make a beautiful quilt."

The corners of Rachel's mouth turned up in a smile and her eyes had a faraway look as she watched Jennifer take the shirts from the basket and put them into her bags. Jennifer looked up when she felt Rachel watching her.

"Are you sure you're ready to part with them?"

Rachel met Jennifer's eyes. "I am now. Talking to you has helped me realize this is the right decision. When they're made into a quilt, I can have it on my bed to look at every day. Otherwise, they'll either get packed away out of sight or eventually given away. I'm just taking one last look at how they are now and thinking about how they'll look when you bring them back to me."

Jennifer nodded. "I understand. I'll try to get it finished as quickly as possible so you can have them back."

"Don't feel pressured to do that. I can wait."

Jennifer tucked the final shirt in a bag and laid it on the couch with the others while she put on her coat. "One more hug?" she asked, stretching out her arms. Rachel stepped into them and the women stood for a moment, ending their visit as they'd begun.

CHAPTER 2

The aroma of turkey soup and freshly baked bread mingled with the scent of brownies in Eva Perkins's kitchen for the weekly potluck supper-slash-quilt club meeting.

"Sarah Pascal, if you try to skip straight to dessert, I'm revoking your quilt privileges," Eva warned when she saw her reaching out to take a brownie.

Sarah snatched her hand back, but grinned, knowing Eva's bark was worse than her bite.

"Yes, ma'am. A brownie isn't worth that."

"It's hard to believe we were strangers, or at the most, just acquaintances, this time last year," Jennifer Ryder said, ladling soup into her bowl.

"Strangers with secrets," Annalise Jordan commented and took the proffered ladle from Jennifer.

"It's been those secrets as much as the quilting that has brought us together," Eva said, when they were all at the dining room table. "I always had to pretend I didn't understand him when I spoke to Reuben in front of other people. I figured they'd think I was just one of *those* people."

The group chuckled, knowing exactly what she meant.

"At least you could act somewhat normal talking to your cat. People aren't quite as forgiving about people talking to ghosts. I definitely had to keep that hidden and I'm honestly not sure if I would have shared that I can do that with Ashley, even though she is my wife. I'm so glad you trusted us enough to out us about our abilities, Annalise, including that you're psychic."

"I didn't even know what you called what I could do," Jennifer said. "Psychometry isn't exactly a household term people in small-town Maine talk about."

"Something else we didn't count on and even I didn't intuit when we met was that we'd be solving six murders," Annalise said, taking another slice of bread and spreading it with butter. "Sometimes even when the police had hit a dead end, no pun intended."

"Do you remember our first meetings with Phil and Dennis? But I can't say that I blame them. Homicide detectives must see a lot in their line of work but it's probably not every day that they're asked to believe how we were able to solve the cases," Eva remarked.

Sarah spurted out the mouthful of soup she'd just taken and began to giggle uncontrollably. She grabbed the folded napkin in front of her and covered her mouth.

"What got you going?" Jennifer asked, smiling.

"I was thinking about the first couple of times they each saw me talking to a ghost," Sarah said, wiping tears from the corners of her eyes with the napkin.

"I would have liked to be there to see that," Jennifer said. Her spoon was halfway to her mouth when she realized what that would mean. "On second thought, maybe I wouldn't."

The others chuckled at her confession.

"The important thing is they kept an open mind and now they've accepted what we do. And I think they consider us a part of their team. Even if they can't write about it in their reports," Annalise said, smiling.

"And because of that we've helped families have closure," Eva said.

"And put those responsible behind bars," Sarah added, serious now.

Annalise raised her water glass. "To secrets, stitches, and solving mysteries."

They clinked their glasses in solidarity, a spark of friendship—and purpose—passing between them.

CHAPTER 3

"Well, ladies, I was afraid the craft fair was going to do us in, but we made it to a new year," Eva said when the club members had finished their dinner and the next part of their weekly meeting began.

"It might have been less stressful if we didn't have another murder on top of making items to sell at the fair," Annalise replied.

"I'm beginning to think we might be bad luck! Have you noticed that there's been a murder every month since we started the quilt club?" Sarah asked leaning forward for emphasis.

"Maybe we should change our name to the Cozy Quilts and Deadly Clues Club. Our tagline could be: *Have a murder to solve? We'll stitch together the clues and catch your killer,*" Eva joked. "Although that might be a little too much exposure to the community. It's been hard enough keeping our paranormal skills under the radar and having to explain that's how we've helped the police arrest six killers already."

"It wasn't a murder, but what I have to say is about someone dying. I visited with Rachel Hartley last week," Jennifer told the group, her tone serious now. "

"Should I know who Rachel Hartley is?" Sarah asked.

"I'm sorry, Sarah, I wasn't thinking that you probably wouldn't recognize the name since you don't live in Glen Lake," Jennifer apologized. "Her husband, Ted, was killed in a hunting accident back in November. Rachel asked if I would make a memory quilt for her using Ted's shirts and wants to use the Hunter's Star pattern. Have any of you ever done one of those? A memory quilt, I mean."

"No, but what a great idea!" Annalise's face lit up. "When I was going through the boxes in my attic this past summer to find my dad's piece of the treasure map, I found some of his clothes that my mom had packed. I think there might be a box with a couple of dresses and an apron of my mother's up there, too. Using them to make a quilt would be such a better way to preserve them."

"You aren't worried it might remind you that you almost ended up being another victim as well as solving our second murder case because of that treasure map, would you?" Sarah asked.

"No. And I wasn't the only one who solved that. It was a group effort," Annalise replied. "And that's assuming the mice haven't gotten to the clothes."

Mice? Reuben had been curled up on Eva's lap, but he lifted his head and his ears perked up at the mention.

Eva looked down at her cat and raised one eyebrow. "You and I both know you don't have the slightest interest in mice, and as far as I know, we don't have any here. Which is a good thing because if I'd planned on you being a mouser, I would have been sorely disappointed."

If I'd known you intended to use me as a mouser, I wouldn't have stayed. I'd say you're the one who would have been disappointed on several counts. The tip of Reuben's tail twitched, and he gave Eva a haughty look as he fired off that final salvo before jumping down from her lap and retiring to the living room to finish his nap.

The other ladies grinned at the exchange, inferring the gist of their conversation.

"I think you hit a nerve," Sarah said, smiling.

"It's not the first time today, and probably not the last. He's been even more prickly than usual, if that's even possible."

"You might be more worried about him if he wasn't prickly," Jennifer teased.

"You may be right."

"Okay, for the newbie quilter, I think I've got the idea, but what's a memory quilt?" Sarah asked, returning them to their original topic.

"It's made using fabric from items that were worn or used by the person whose memories you want to save. They don't always have to be for someone who's died. Some people make them from clothing or blankets children had when they were young and then gift it to them when they're older," Jennifer explained.

Sarah nodded her head in understanding. "I wonder if Vivian still has any of Lily's clothes. I bet she would love the idea of making them into a quilt. And Meghan, too, but I don't know if I would have time to make two even if she does have them. "

"I'd be happy to help you," Eva offered. "I don't really have anyone myself who I'd like to make one for. How are Vivian and Meghan doing since Lily died?"

"Meghan moved out of their apartment a month after we solved Lily's murder and she and Panda are happier in their new place. I don't speak Cat, so you'd have to ask him to know for sure. She said it was too hard staying there because every time she went into the kitchen, she would think about finding Lily's body. Even though we caught her killer and I told her Lily was at peace, she couldn't get comfortable. I haven't heard from Vivian a lot since then, but we've talked a few times and she seems to be doing better."

"That's good to hear. Why don't you check with them and if

they like the idea of a memory quilt and have some of Lily's clothes, I'd be happy to help you with the project."

"Thanks, Eva. I'll let you know. We might even have to take a trip to Quilting Essentials to buy more fabric and batting," Sarah said, and gave Eva a wink. It was a running joke about their finding excuses to go shopping for material, even when they had plenty in their stashes.

"And you know you wouldn't have to twist my arm," Eva said with a smile.

"My head is spinning with ideas. I'm not looking forward to going into my unheated attic in January, but it will be worth it to finally put my mom and dad's old clothes to good use," Annalise said.

"It sounds like we've got this month's quilt project decided. Same time, same place next week, ladies?" Eva asked.

"Can't wait!" Jennifer said, and the others nodded in agreement.

CHAPTER 4

"Come on, Nicky, we're going to be late." Matt Ryder stood in the kitchen with his backpack slung over one shoulder, a slight scowl on his face. "I'm going out now to start the car and if you're not there in two minutes, I'm leaving without you and you can take the bus."

"I'm coming. I'm coming," she shouted from the bathroom. "I can't leave with mascara on just one eye. Mom, tell him he's got to wait."

Jennifer rolled her eyes at her husband, David, who was finishing up his breakfast at their kitchen table.

"Nicky, you need to get a move on. You can put your mascara on in the car if you haven't finished. Both of you need to get to school on time."

"Fine! I'm coming!" Nicky's footsteps pounded down the hallway and a glowering sixteen-year-old appeared in the kitchen, where she grabbed the lunch Jennifer had prepared and stuffed it into her unzipped backpack.

A cold rush of air floated into the room when Matt opened the front door.

A look of panic came over Nicky's face as she struggled into her winter coat. "Matt, wait. Don't leave without me!" She snatched up her backpack and ran down the stairs after her brother. "Bye, Mom. Bye, Dad," she called out almost as an afterthought before slamming the door behind her.

Their Jack Russell terrier, Boscoe, looked up from his bed in the corner of the kitchen and gave a single bark in reply.

"Remind me again about how we're going to miss this when they're gone," Jennifer said, smiling at her husband.

"Enjoy it while you can. Only a couple more years and they'll both have flown the nest."

David walked to the dishwasher and put in his breakfast dishes. "Anything special on your to do list for your day off?"

"I'm going to start the quilt for Rachel. I've got the pattern, but I have to sort out the shirts and figure out how much fabric I'll need to buy to make sure I have enough."

"Sounds like fun!"

"It's going to be even more fun now that I have a dedicated spot for my sewing. I still can't believe how nice it turned out. And thank you! It was the best Christmas present ever."

"You're welcome. I know how important the quilting has been for you. The kids might not be happy about giving up some of the rec room space, but they'll live," David smiled and leaned over to give Jennifer a kiss on the cheek. "I'd better get going, too. Unless something comes up that I wasn't expecting, I should be home on time, but I'll call if it does." He took his coat from the closet in the hallway and popped his head into the kitchen to blow her a kiss before descending the stairs to the basement garage in their raised ranch home.

"What do you think, Boscoe? Do you want to come downstairs and keep me company while I work?"

Hearing his name, the dog lifted his head from his bed and glanced at Jennifer and then plopped it back down and closed his eyes.

"Alrighty, then. You know where to find me if you change your mind."

Jennifer bent down to stroke the top of Boscoe's head and he rewarded her with a contented sigh before she headed to the rec room.

I can't believe how lucky I am, she thought as she walked toward the tall cabinet tucked against the far wall of the room. She opened the doors and folded them back so they expanded to their full width. It was large enough to hold all her supplies, cloth, and tools, as well as her sewing machine, and also had a fold-down tabletop extension she used to cut fabric.

"Let's see what we've got here," she said aloud, despite being alone except for Boscoe, who was still upstairs. She sat cross-legged on the floor and dumped the contents of all the bags she'd brought home from Rachel's in front of her. It had already been a week since their visit, with all of Jennifer's family and work commitments taking priority. As she picked up a blue chambray from the bottom of the pile, she felt a connection, signaling that her psychometry was kicking in, and the world around her faded into the background. She was no longer in the rec room. She was in a small clearing surrounded by trees.

She was looking at a pair of orange leather-gloved hands reaching for the rungs of a ladder. Through the spaces between the rungs, she saw tree bark. *Has to be a man from the size of the hands.* The thought flitted into her consciousness and then her focus immediately shifted back to what she was seeing. He had reached the top of the ladder and was stepping onto a wooden platform. And then a loud creak and her heart began to race. She experienced the sensation of movement under her/his feet, and drew in her breath as she experienced his panic when the structure gave way entirely, catapulting him to the ground. Her stomach lurched. A flash of sky. Mere seconds later there was only blackness, but Jennifer's vision continued.

She heard footsteps crunching in the snow and felt the presence of someone leaning in. A deep, rough voice, satisfied.

"Worked out just like I planned it."

Footsteps again, retreating this time, and then silence enveloped her as her heart hammered in her chest. The vision's hold on her released its grip, and she was back in her rec room. She shivered involuntarily and sat staring at the shirt in her lap, her hands still holding it by the shoulders, but now they were trembling.

Ted was murdered. She let that thought settle. *Now what do I do? I can't tell Rachel. She'd think I'm crazy.* Right on its heels came the thought *I've got to tell the Club.*

She put the shirt aside and forced herself to place her attention on the task she'd set out to do when she came downstairs. She heard a soft *woof!* behind her and turned to see Boscoe looking at her with concern in his eyes.

"It's okay, buddy. *I'm* okay. C'mere so I can give you a hug."

Boscoe trotted over and she wrapped her arms around his neck, as much to ground herself in reality as to reassure him.

"Why don't you stay awhile and keep me company? I'll bring your bed over next to me." Without waiting for a reply—after all, she wasn't Eva—she hopped up and pulled the cushion close to her but far enough away so she wouldn't trip over him, and sat back on the floor. He gave her another look as though deciding whether she was really okay, as she'd said, and then laid down with his chin on his front paws, his eyes glued to her.

Jennifer took a deep breath and continued the sorting and calculating how many of the shirts she'd be able to use, all the time avoiding the blue chambray. As she concentrated on her task, the anxiety she'd felt faded, but lingered in her subconscious.

———

"I have something I need to tell you."

David had just come out of their en suite bathroom where he'd been brushing his teeth and was now dressed in his pajama bottoms and a tee shirt.

"Oh?" he said guardedly, as he pulled back the covers and climbed into bed beside her.

"I had a vision when I was sorting Ted's clothes."

David's eyebrows lifted almost imperceptibly, but he waited for her to continue.

"I think I was holding the shirt he was wearing the day he died."

David's eyebrows rose even higher this time. By now, he'd become more comfortable about Jennifer's psychometry, but her body language told him this would not be good news.

"Okay. What did you see?"

"Ted wasn't alone when it happened. A man walked into the woods and checked his pulse after Ted fell. And when they knew he was dead, they just left. Dave, it wasn't an accident. The person who was there said *It worked out just like I planned it.* I think someone tampered with the platform."

"You're sure?" he finally said.

"Yeah. I never saw the other person, but I know Ted was aware of what he said. I can't explain it. It's just a certainty I feel when the visions are true."

"Are you going to talk to Phil and Dennis? It's already been ruled an accident, so it's a closed case."

"Not yet. I want to discuss this with the ladies first."

He nodded his understanding. "Good idea. And, Jen," he leveled his eyes with hers. "Be careful. All of you."

CHAPTER 5

"I'm so excited to show you what I've done so far," Annalise exclaimed at the Club's next meeting as she spread out her project at her sewing station in Eva's studio. "I got lucky and found the boxes with my mom and dad's things before hypothermia set in. I had my winter coat, a hat, and gloves on, but it's still cold up in the attic. I really need to get that insulated better." She glanced up to see three sets of eyes watching her expectantly. "Sorry, got sidetracked. Anyway, there weren't as many clothes as I'd hoped, but I think I can make a good-sized wall hanging from what I unearthed without having to add much--and maybe no--extra fabric. I'm going to do a landscape of the house instead of a quilt design. They loved that place and made so many happy memories there. Here's the sketch of what I have planned."

"Oh, Annalise, that's going to be a perfect tribute. You're so artistic! But I don't see any purple shutters and the door is white," Sarah said.

"Those weren't original to the house. My parents would never have gone for purple, so that came when I took over the house."

"What a great way to honor them and now you'll have another piece of art to display. Where do you think you'll put it?" Eva asked.

"I haven't decided yet whether it will be the living room or my Reiki studio. I think my clients would appreciate it, but I'll see how it turns out first."

"I called Vivian to ask about Lily's clothes and she still had the box Meghan sent to her. She shipped them back to me overnight, so I brought them with me tonight. She was really excited about having a quilt made from them and thought there was enough if I wanted to do something for Meghan, too. I was on the fence about asking her, but when I told her the idea, she was thrilled. So, I guess that means you've got a project now, too, Eva. They both thought they would like a throw size. I'll need some help from all of you to figure out how to cut them up to get the most yardage."

"Have you picked out patterns yet?" Eva asked.

"I searched for ones that had the word lily in them and finally decided on Carolina Lily for each of them. Even though it's the same, they will look completely different because we won't be using the same clothes. I've got the instructions and how much fabric is required right here." She pulled two totes filled with clothing from her rolling tote and placed them on the table and then removed a printout of the pattern from one of the bags. "I separated the pieces I want to use for each of them, so these clothes are for Vivian's and these are for Meghan's," she said, pointing at each bag respectively.

"I think we should be able to figure it out and if we can't, we can go to Quilting Essentials and Evelyn can help us," Eva said, taking the printouts from Sarah. She was about to begin when she realized Jennifer had been quiet this entire time. "Jen, are you alright? I know you already have your project planned, but you haven't said a word. That's not like you."

"I was going to say something earlier, but everyone's been so excited, I didn't want to spoil the mood. When I was sorting out Ted's clothes I had a vision, and I'm sure it was real because of how strongly I reacted to it. I was seeing what happened the day he died, and the platform didn't collapse by accident. I'm convinced it was sabotaged. Ted was murdered."

CHAPTER 6

The room fell into stunned silence.

"What did you see that makes you think that?" Annalise was the first to speak after the initial shock of Jennifer's news.

"It wasn't what I saw. It was what I heard. After he landed on the ground…." Jennifer shivered at the memory. "…. I heard a man's voice saying it had worked out just as he planned."

"Did you recognize the voice?" Sarah asked.

"No, but I had the feeling that Ted did."

"Should we tell Phil and Dennis?" Eva asked.

"We don't have enough information for them yet," Annalise replied.

"Yet?" Sarah asked. "So much for a month without a murder! I must have jinxed us." Her shoulders slumped and she let out an enormous sigh.

Eva laid her hand on Sarah's shoulder to comfort her. "Ted's death had already happened at least two months before you said that. If we're finding out about it, it must mean we're meant to help."

"That's what I think, too," Annalise said.

"I agree, but where do we go from here? I can't think of a

way to bring this up with Rachel. She'd think I was playing some cruel joke on her. And I definitely don't want to upset her by asking questions that would raise her suspicions about why I'd be asking them."

"We've been here before and we've always figured it out. My spidey senses are telling me we'll do it this time, too." Annalise said, her tone confident.

"And in the meantime, let's get back to our happy place….quilting," Eva suggested.

CHAPTER 7

"I had an interesting meeting last night with the quilt club," Eva began her conversation the next day with her partner, Jim Davis. They were having lunch at the Checkout Diner, Glen Lake's only eating establishment, and the town's unofficial social center.

"Oh? Do say," Jim replied.

Eva looked around the room to make sure no one was eavesdropping and lowered her voice as an extra measure. "Jen is making Rachel Hartley a memory quilt from Ted's shirts and when she was holding one of them, she had a vision."

Jim was one of the first people outside of their immediate circle who learned about the ladies' paranormal abilities, so telling him Jennifer had a vision didn't surprise him. He simply nodded for Eva to continue.

"Jen believes Ted's death wasn't an accident. It was deliberate. We're stumped for how we can figure this out, though. Do you have any ideas?"

He'd been a state trooper before he retired, which made him a good choice as a sounding board.

Jim took a bite of his cheeseburger and thought for a moment. "Ted was a private investigator. It could have something to do with one of his cases. Maybe he got too close to finding out information that had consequences for the killer if it was revealed. He was well-liked in the community from what I knew of him, so that's the only explanation I can think of."

"It's a good one. It would explain a lot. Now we just need to figure out who he was investigating."

"And how do you intend to…. No, don't tell me. I'd rather have plausible deniability."

"That's easy. We don't have a plan, which is why I was hoping you could help."

Jim cringed, hearing the annoyance in Eva's voice, but was rescued by Betty Jones coming to the table to refill their coffee mugs.

As she was pouring, she asked, "Is there anything else I can get you now? We've got chocolate cake, just made this morning, if you're in the mood for something sweet."

Eva was about to say she'd pass on the dessert, but inspiration hit and she took a chance asking Betty about what she might know about Ted. Betty heard all the gossip in town and wasn't shy about sharing it.

"Did Ted Hartley ever meet any of his clients here? The Club is making a memory quilt for Rachel and we thought it might make it even more special to include messages from friends and associates of Ted's when we give it to her." She hoped the innocent expression she put on her face was believable.

"Well, isn't that nice? He would bring people in for lunch sometimes. I can't say for sure if they were clients or just friends who don't live in Glen Lake."

"Was he here with anyone recently who you hadn't seen before? We already have the obvious choices." Betty didn't need to know that wasn't true.

Betty looked up as she held the coffee pot in one hand and her other hand on her hip as she thought. "There was one fella he brought in about a month, I think, before his accident. His name was Henry something." Her eyebrows scrunched together in concentration. "Henry Ward. That was it!" she announced triumphantly. "Nice guy. I don't think he lives in town or I would have seen him before. He probably wouldn't be who you're looking for. So, what's the verdict on the cake?" she asked, making it obvious that was all she had to say about Ted.

"How about you bring one piece and two forks? I'm watching my waistline, so I'll share with Eva." He patted his stomach and gave Betty a conspiratorial wink.

"Coming right up!" Betty bustled off to the kitchen.

"Do you know him?" Eva asked as soon as the coast was clear.

"Henry Ward?"

"Yes! Who else?" Eva scowled at him.

Oops, Buddy, I think you crossed the 'I've lost my patience with you' line with that one. He grinned broadly to ease the tension. "Settle down. I'm just teasing."

She huffed and tried to remain angry, but softened when he gently squeezed her hand.

"Okay, I may have overreacted, but this is serious and you haven't answered my question. Do you know Henry Ward?" Her voice was softer this time.

"Well, I don't know if it's the same one, but there's a Henry Ward in Bangor who's an accountant. There was a rumor that he was connected to criminal activities, but nothing was ever proven, and I think he got away from those clients."

"I wonder if that had anything to do with why he was meeting with Ted. That would make sense as to why they were in Glen Lake instead of Bangor," Eva said, more to herself than to Jim.

Betty arrived with a gigantic piece of chocolate cake, two plates, and two forks.

"That might be a little bigger portion than we normally serve. It's the *regular customer slice* size, but keep that under your hat." She gave them a sly smile, put the tab on the table, and walked away.

Eva looked longingly at the cake, internally battling the debate about whether to resist or stick to her New Year's resolution to lose weight.

"You only live once, right?" she asked Jim rhetorically and divided it into two unequal pieces with one of the forks. She slid the smaller section onto a plate and took a bite. Her eyes closed in bliss and she hummed an *mmm* as she savored the flavor of the rich chocolate layers and chocolate ganache topping.

"That was worth every single calorie," she said, and then slid the fork between her pursed lips to remove the last bit of cake and frosting before placing it on her empty plate.

Jim chuckled. "Looks like that hit the spot. Are you sure you don't want a piece of your own? I can have Betty wrap it up for you to take home."

"Yes, I *want* it, but I don't *need* it, so no, thank you. I'm ready to go."

Once they settled into Jim's car, Eva played Jim's words about Henry Ward back in her head and a thought occurred to her.

"Do you think you could ask your buddies who are still on the force what they know about Henry Ward? I can't shake the feeling that he's one of the pieces of the puzzle."

Jim glanced over at her and saw the determination in her eyes. He knew that look.

"Okay, I can't promise anything, but I'll see what I can do. What should I say if they want to know why I'm asking?"

She smiled coyly. "You were a cop. I'm sure you can figure out something."

CHAPTER 8

Eva juggled a plate of scones in one hand and knocked at Rachel's door with the other. A dog barked from somewhere inside the house, but nothing resembling a human coming to answer the door. She was about to knock again when she heard footsteps approaching. The door opened and Eva was met with a look of surprise.

"Eva, how nice to see you! Come in out of the cold." Rachel stood aside to give Eva room to enter.

"I hope I'm not intruding. It's been too long since we've gotten together, but I wanted to give you some space. I brought scones!" She held up the plate and struggled to remove her jacket.

"Let me take those for you," Rachel said, retrieving the dish before Eva dropped it. "I'm so glad you came. I should have called you sooner, but..."

"You don't have to apologize. I understand." Eva hung her coat on an empty peg in the row of pegs mounted to the wall and then extended her arms. "Here, give me a hug. I've missed you."

Now it was Rachel's turn to juggle the plate, but Eva was

relieved to see a genuine smile on her face when they broke the embrace.

"Let's go in the kitchen. These scones look delicious."

"Well, hello, Finn. How are you doing today?" Eva greeted the Hartleys' spaniel with a scratch under his chin when he trotted over to her from his bed in the corner.

I'm not as sad, but I still miss Ted.

Eva bent her head down close to Finn's ear so Rachel wouldn't hear, and whispered, "I know. We all do, and I promise it will get better with time."

Finn whined softly and licked Eva's hand, looking up at her with his sad eyes, before going back to his bed.

Eva took a seat at the banquette as Rachel got two plates from the open shelving and brought them to the table. "Coffee? I just made a fresh pot. Or I can put the kettle on if you'd rather have tea."

"Coffee will do just fine, and a splash of half and half if you have it."

"Coming right up."

"Jennifer is so excited about the memory quilt for Ted. And before you apologize for not asking me, I want you to know that I'm not in the least bit offended. Jennifer will do a wonderful job with it and I've volunteered to help one of the other ladies in our quilt group because she has two people she's making quilts for."

"I admit I was a little worried, but I thought you'd understand." Rachel smiled warmly. "We sure do miss you at school, Eva, and so do the parents who were hoping you'd be their children's teacher."

"There are times when I miss teaching and the kids. But I've missed being around the other teachers, too. It was such fun when we were working at the same school. At least I'm lucky enough to have you living next door. If you're ever having a bad day, feel free to vent to me. It will be cathartic for both of us. You can get it off your chest and it will remind me of why I don't miss all the paperwork that comes with the job."

Rachel snorted and nearly choked on her coffee. "You've got that right. I've got a pile of papers to grade this weekend. In fact, that's what I was doing when you knocked, but I'm delighted about the interruption… and your company and these scones. They're delicious!"

"I'm happy to share the calories. I was supposed to be on a diet, but it's yet another year with my New Year's resolution broken before February. And if you don't mind my saying so, it looks like you can use the extra calories. I know you must be tired of being asked, but how are you doing, dear?" Eva covered Rachel's hand with hers.

Rachel's eyes watered and she sighed.

"Some days I think I'm getting better and then it hits me all over again. I keep thinking of Ted lying there on the ground and all alone. He was supposed to be hunting with Vinnie Barnes, but Vinnie came out to see Ted at his office a few days before. Ted told me he came to let him know he had to cancel. You know Ted, he'd be out every day he could during deer season, so he decided to go by himself."

At the mention of Vinnie Barnes, Finn growled low in his throat, catching Eva's attention, but she'd have to wait for a better time to ask him to elaborate. Her mind raced. *This could be a clue. Try not to sound like you're being nosey with Rachel and find a way to talk to him.*

"I don't think I know Vinnie Barnes. Was he an old friend of Ted's?"

"No, actually, they just met a couple of months ago through a mutual friend. Henry Ward introduced them. Henry was Ted's accountant for the business, but they were friends, too."

That could explain why Henry was meeting with Ted at the Diner, but this can't be a coincidence. I'm going to ask Jim about this Vinnie Barnes, too.

"Carl Tremblay was the one who notified me. He said the EMTs told him it happened quickly. I'm not sure how they know that, but it helps a little to believe Ted didn't suffer."

"I've met Deputy Tremblay. He strikes me as a kind man and someone who has a lot of compassion. I'm glad he was the one who came to notify you."

Rachel hesitated.

"I've never said this to anyone else, but I know I can trust you, Eva. I can't explain it, but I've had this feeling that it wasn't an accident." She looked into Eva's eyes and leaned her forearms on the table, her hands clasped tightly together. "Maybe it's just that I can't accept that Ted's death was random. I know I'm sounding crazy or desperate to rationalize why this happened. I'm sorry…. please excuse me for a moment."

Before Eva could say anything, Rachel shoved back in her chair and bolted from the room and into the bathroom, closing the door behind her.

Eva watched Rachel's retreating back. *This is your chance.* She walked over to Finn and leaned down with her back to the hallway where Rachel had departed.

"Finn, tell me about Vinnie Barnes. What upset you when Rachel mentioned his name?"

I didn't know his name then, but I was sleeping under Ted's desk when the bad man came into the office, so he didn't know I was there. He started yelling at Ted and they got into a fight. He said he knew what Ted was doing. Ted said he didn't know what the bad man was talking about and then the bad man told Ted he would make him pay. That's when he left. I could tell Ted was upset. He called someone and said, We have to talk. He's onto me. That's all he said, so I don't think he was talking to a real person.

"Do you mean he was leaving a message?"

Yes. A voice mail? Is that what humans call it?

"That's right."

Finn whined and his eyes shifted. *She's coming back.*

Eva stroked Finn's head and whispered, "Thank you, Finn. That was important," before standing to greet Rachel.

"I'm so sorry…" Rachel began. Her eyes were red and puffy.

"Don't be," Eva interrupted and took her in her arms. "And I don't think you're crazy," she said softly. "We should all trust our intuition more. It's usually right. If this wasn't an accident, the truth will come out. I believe that with all my heart."

Eva could feel Rachel nodding her head against her shoulder and gave her another squeeze before releasing her.

"I should go home and let you get back to your grading. And I meant what I said, if there's anything you ever want to talk about, I'm right next door."

She retrieved her coat and turned to Rachel with one hand on the doorknob and said, "About what you said… about thinking it might not have been an accident… I believe you."

Rachel's eyes searched Eva's face for any sign of doubt and once she was convinced there was none, nodded her response.

CHAPTER 9

"Eva, it's good to see you," Evelyn Jackson greeted her as she entered Quilting Essentials. "What can I do for you today?"

Eva held up the bag in her hand.

"Sarah Pascal is meeting me here. The Club has decided to make memory quilts this month and we're going to be making a throw for two of Sarah's friends. Do you remember hearing about Lily Sullivan's murder a couple of months ago?"

"Was she the one who turned out to be an informant for the DEA?"

"Yes, that's the one. One of Sarah's good friends was her roommate. We're going to be using some of Lily's clothes, but we'll need to add more fabric to make two throw quilts from this pattern."

A chime sounded, and both women turned toward the door where Sarah was entering.

"Sorry, time got away from me this morning. Have you been waiting long?" Sarah asked Eva.

"I just got here myself. I was telling Evelyn about our projects."

"Jennifer told me she's doing a memory quilt for Rachel

Hartley. She was in last week to get more background and backing material," Evelyn said.

"That's what got me thinking about making these. Well, me and Eva, since she volunteered to help me out," Sarah said. "I hadn't heard about memory quilts before. I might need to book time to use the longarm machine once I get the top done."

"Of course, just let me know when you're ready," Evelyn replied. "It's so sad about Ted. I haven't seen Rachel since his funeral. How is she doing?"

"As well as can be expected, but it's still early days. It takes time to get over something like this, but I think the quilt is a step toward healing."

"It was such a strange thing to happen. I didn't want to cause Rachel any distress by asking, but did you hear anything about how it happened? Ted was an experienced hunter and if it was a tree stand he had used before, he should have known whether it was safe," Evelyn said.

Eva and Sarah exchanged furtive glances, but knew they couldn't say more.

"I haven't asked Rachel about specifics. I'd heard it was ruled an accident, so assumed the authorities had looked into it," Eva said, crossing her fingers.

"There's talk around town that he was friends with Vinnie Barnes. There have been rumors for years about him being *connected*. Ted could have gotten on Vinnie's bad side and who knows what would happen if he did." Evelyn let the implication hang in the air, but Eva and Sarah weren't taking the bait.

"I shouldn't take too long. I have to get back to a project for work," Sarah said to divert attention. "We were hoping you could tell us how much material we'll need to get for this pattern," she said, removing it from the bag with Lily's clothes. "Could we use one of the tables in the classroom to spread things out?"

"Oh, sure. There's nothing going on there now," Evelyn said and turned to walk to the back of the store.

Sarah and Eva exchanged glances, both with their eyebrows raised, before following her.

"Do you think someone knows more about this?" Sarah whispered.

"Hard to say. There are always rumors flying in Glen Lake. But when I visited Rachel yesterday, she mentioned Vinnie Barnes. He and Ted were supposed to go hunting together the day Ted died and their dog, Finn, said he heard him threaten Ted. I think we'll need to keep our eyes and ears open just in case there's more to this."

CHAPTER 10

"I've got the information you asked for," Jim announced as he sliced a cucumber for their salad.

"About Henry Ward?" Eva asked, adding romaine to the bowl.

"Yup. My buddies didn't have a lot to say but what I got was that Henry used to work for Vinnie Barnes but went out on his own a few years ago. This is pretty much what I told you at the diner. Within the past year, though, the word on the street is that he's working for him again, just not as an employee."

"Do they know why he went back with Vinnie? If he left because he didn't want to be associated with him, doesn't it seem odd that he'd do it at all? There's even more at risk if it meant he'd lose his entire business." Eva speculated.

"That's what I thought, too. When I pressed my source on it, he pretended he had no idea, but my gut is telling me there's more to it."

"Listen to you. My *source*. You sound like something right out of a TV show," she teased.

Jim chuckled but kept his head bent, intent on his sous chef tasks. "That should do it for the salad," he said dropping a handful of cherry tomatoes into the bowl.

"Sarah and I were at Quilting Essentials this afternoon and Ted's accident came up because we were talking about Rachel's quilt. Evelyn said something we thought was interesting and might be significant."

"Oh? What was that?"

"Apparently there are rumors going around town that Ted might have stepped on Vinnie's toes. Some people are speculating it wasn't an accident." Eva said.

"You know how it is in small towns, Eva. If life gets too boring, people feel like they have to spice things up by starting rumors."

"That's what we thought, too. But you know the old saying, where's there's smoke, there's fire. Maybe whoever started the rumor knows more than they're letting on."

"Good luck tracking that down," Jim replied, but in a tone that indicated he didn't think that would happen.

Eva's shoulders slumped. "You're probably right." She turned to put the bowl of mashed potatoes on the island where they would be eating and caught a movement out of the corner of her eye. "Did you just give him a piece of chicken?" she demanded.

"Oops, she's onto us, buddy," Jim said, guiltily.

"You know he's not supposed to be getting any treats," Eva chastised.

"But it's chicken. It's good protein," he said. The look on Eva's face let him know she wasn't buying it. "Sorry, it won't happen again. Cross my heart," Jim told her earnestly, but gave Reuben a wink.

Reuben was too busy devouring the chicken before Eva had a chance to take it away from him to notice. When he swallowed it, he gave her a smug look of satisfaction and padded away.

"Sure. Make me the bad guy when all I'm trying to do is keep him healthy," she grumbled.

Jim kissed her cheek. "This time I mean it. It won't happen again," he said, holding out his arms for a hug.

Eva continued scowling at him but then sighed and let him take her in his arms.

CHAPTER 11

"Hey, are you alright? You seem preoccupied." Liam Campbell lightly squeezed Annalise's hand. "You've been picking at your food and haven't said a word for the last five minutes. It's okay to tell me if you don't like it. I won't make you clean your plate before you can have dessert," he teased.

"I'm sorry. It's not the food. The carbonara is delicious and I can't believe how lucky I am to have found someone who's not only handsome and a talented potter, but can cook like a Michelin chef."

"Then what's going on? Maybe I can help."

She smiled wanly. "It's a dream I had last night. It's been haunting me all day."

He cocked his head slightly. "Want to tell me about it?"

This could get complicated if he keeps pushing, she thought. *But if you stay in this relationship—and you know that's what you want--the truth is bound to come out, and it's better that happens sooner than later.* Her decision made, she took a deep, steadying breath.

"I dreamed that Eva's neighbor's office was broken into. It was night... maybe middle of the night. The office is on their property but in a separate building next to their house. The intruder was looking for something and files were scattered everywhere. When they didn't find what they wanted in those, they took his laptop. Their dog heard them and started barking, which woke up the neighbor's wife, but the intruder was already leaving. That's when I woke up."

"Well, I can see how that would be upsetting, but it seems like a disproportionate reaction. It was just a dream."

"That's just it, Liam. Sometimes… a lot of times… my dreams come true." Annalise leveled her eyes on Liam's and held her breath.

He was quiet as he returned her gaze.

He's going to tell me to leave and never come back.

"I knew it! You're psychic, aren't you?"

Annalise's mouth dropped. *I was not expecting that!*

"What… what makes you think that?"

"Little things you've said and how you seem to know me so well. Almost as though you can read my thoughts," he said, and paused. "But even if you are, I'm okay with that. It doesn't frighten me. We haven't talked much about the *woo woo* topics, but I like to think I've got a pretty open mind. So, tell me more."

Annalise blinked as if awakening from a dream.

"Wow." She let out her breath and her shoulders relaxed. "You just keep getting better and better. You're right, I have a gift. It's not something I share with anyone unless I know I can trust them. There's more about this dream that has me so worried. The person who owns the office is dead. He died a couple months ago in what they ruled an accident, but it was murder. He was…"

"Wait. Back up the bus. Why do you think it was murder?" Liam asked.

Uh oh, that was a mistake. I can't tell him about Jennifer's vision without giving away her secret.

"You'll have to trust me on that one for now. I promise when I can, I'll tell you, but in the meantime, I can tell you this. He was a private investigator and I believe the intruder was looking for evidence that would incriminate them. What I'm really wrestling with is whether I should try to warn his wife. I'm certain she wasn't harmed in any way, so I don't think she's in danger. But am I being too cautious because I have no idea how to tell her this without having her think I'm crazy? I can't have it spread around town that I'm pretending to be psychic. It could ruin my Reiki practice."

He nodded his head.

"I see your dilemma. You're absolutely convinced she wasn't harmed?"

"Yes."

"Are you ever wrong?"

"Sometimes, but I can tell the difference between a premonition and just a dream. This is a premonition. I'm positive of it."

"Then perhaps silence is the way to go. It's a good bet she'll call 911 and my guess is they would make extra patrols for a while to make sure she's safe. Even if the intruder couldn't find what they were looking for there, chances are they won't come back. What would be the point? Or maybe the police will figure out who it was and arrest them."

"Yeah, you're probably right. Thanks for the advice. And not tossing me out the door because you think I'm a kook," she said, smiling. But inside, the doubt continued. *I need to talk to Eva. First thing tomorrow.*

CHAPTER 12

"You're up bright and early!" Eva said upon answering her phone.

"And hello to you, too," Annalise teased. "Are you free this morning? I have something I want to run by you."

"Free as a bird. What time's good for you?"

"How about now? I don't want to wait any longer and I want to talk it over with you before the Club meeting tonight."

"Now's good. I'll put a pot of coffee on and I made blueberry muffins this morning."

"You had me at coffee. I'll see you in fifteen."

Annalise is here, Reuben announced when her car pulled into Eva's driveway. *She looks upset. She must have had one of her visions.*

He said this just as Eva walked past him on her way to the door.

"If cats could do air quotes, I'd swear you would have just then. Don't you be dissing Annalise's gift. You know her visions come true."

And if I could roll my eyes, that's what you'd be seeing now.

Eva gave him a side eye and opened the door.

"So, what has you in a dither this morning?" Eva asked once they settled in at her dining room table.

"I had a dream two nights ago about Rachel. Well, really about Ted's office. It was broken into, and I think the intruder was looking for some sort of evidence. I'm convinced it's connected to Ted's death. Rachel wasn't hurt, but Finn woke her up just as they were leaving."

"Do you think they'll come back?" Eva asked, her brow furrowed.

"I didn't get that impression." She paused, weighing how much she wanted to say. "I told Liam about the dream. And that I'm psychic."

"NO!" Eva's eyes were round as saucers. "What did he say?"

"You won't believe this, but he said he already suspected it. It's like a weight has been lifted from me now that I don't have to hide it from him anymore."

Eva nodded. "That's exactly how I felt after I let Jim know I can communicate with animals. He wasn't that easy to convince, though. I was holding my breath the entire time I was in the sunroom waiting for him to tell Reuben his secret. And then when he called me back in and I repeated it after Reuben told me, I was afraid he was going to have a stroke from the look on his face." Eva began to chuckle at the memory now that the worry of Jim having a stroke was behind her.

"It wasn't anything close to that dramatic with Liam. Thank goodness!" Annalise said.

"Do you have any sense of when this might happen?"

"That's the frustrating part. That detail is still fuzzy. It could be next week, next month, or tonight. The break in was at night and there was no moon, so I couldn't see any landmarks like snow on the ground."

"It's going to be an interesting meeting tonight. I have news to share, too. I visited Rachel yesterday and her dog, Finn, shared some information that I think will shed some light on who is involved with Ted's murder."

Now it was Annalise whose face reflected surprise.

"Why don't I tell you now so you'll have some time to think it over and maybe by tonight you'll have ideas to share with the others."

"Yes, please! I don't think I could get through the day without being totally distracted."

Once Eva finished, both women sat silently, each in their own thoughts.

"I was wrong. I'm still going to be distracted," Annalise said with a smile. "Tonight's meeting can't come soon enough."

CHAPTER 13

Jennifer narrowed her eyes at Eva and Annalise as they cleared the last bites of dessert from their plates. "You two look like you've swallowed a canary." Her voice was light and teasing but her curiosity was clearly piqued.

Annalise and Eva exchanged a glance in an unspoken "who goes first?" kind of way. Eva was the first to cave.

"I haven't told you this yet, Jen, but I visited Rachel the other day," she began, fiddling with the fork on her plate as though stalling for time to find the words. "And… I think she might be a little psychic, too."

Jennifer blinked. "Rachel? As in Rachel Hartley?"

Eva nodded. "She admitted she doesn't have anything solid to go on. But she told me—and this was completely unsolicited—that she doesn't think Ted's death was an accident. It's just a gut feeling she has."

"No way," Jennifer exclaimed, setting her fork down slowly.

"Way," Eva replied, raising her brows for effect. "And there's more—she said Ted was supposed to go hunting with someone named Vinnie Barnes. The moment she said his name, Finn started growling."

"What did Rachel do when she heard that?" Sarah asked, leaning in.

"I don't think Rachel even noticed, or maybe she brushed it off. But as soon as she left the room to use the bathroom, I asked him about it."

Jennifer leaned forward now, too, eyes wide with anticipation.

"He told me," Eva continued, "that the *bad man*—those were his words, not mine—had a fight with Ted. He said he'd make him pay if he didn't stop his investigation."

"Whoa," Sarah said.

Jennifer sat back in her chair, absorbing the gravity of that.

"I wonder if that's whose voice I heard," Jennifer said, quietly.

Eva smacked her forehead. "That's right! The deep, rough voice in your vision. I totally forgot about that. Darn it. I could have asked Finn if he could describe the voice. That's all I had time to ask before Rachel came back, but I think that's all he had to say anyway."

She took a breath and gestured to Annalise. "Okay, your turn."

Annalise shifted in her seat, her eyes downcast and her fingers playing with the edge of her napkin. "I had another dream. Someone had broken into Ted's office—the one next door at their house. The intruder didn't try to go in their house but I'm convinced this is related to Ted's murder in some way."

She paused to glance at the others before continuing. "But now I don't know if we should tell Rachel. I mean, how do I explain that I *know* things without admitting I'm psychic? I don't know her that well, and she's still fragile. Eva asked if I thought Rachel might be in danger, and honestly... I don't think so. I've been trying to listen to my gut all day. No alarm bells were set off, but I don't know. There's a lot at stake either way."

She looked from Sarah to Jennifer, "What do you two think?"

They exchanged a look, then spoke in unison.

"Don't tell her."

Jennifer smirked at Sarah. "Jinx, you owe me a coke."

Sarah rolled her eyes but smiled, and the tension in the room lifted just a bit.

"Oh, my gosh, I almost forgot this, too," Eva said.

You know what they say, the mind's the first thing to go.

Eva jumped, making the other women stare at her perplexedly. "I didn't realize you were sitting there," she said to her cat. Reuben had been curled up on one of the spare dining room chairs tucked under the table out of sight.

"Reuben just told me the mind's the first thing to go," Eva explained, as Reuben sat up, giving her his best Cheshire cat smile. "So, before I was so rudely interrupted." She turned to glare at the cat. "I learned that Betty Jones had seen Henry Ward at the Diner with Ted not long before he died. Jim doesn't know him, but told me there were rumors about Henry being connected to shady business. He asked a cop friend about it and confirmed that Henry had left for a while but was back in cahoots with Vinnie again."

"Why don't I do a background check on both of them and see what I can find out," Sarah offered. Her skills as a cyber security analyst had provided clues they used to solve some of their other murder investigations.

"That's a great idea, Sarah," Jennifer complimented.

"And before anyone suggests it, let me stop you now. I am not tromping out into the woods in the middle of January to connect with Ted even if we did know where the tree stand is located," she announced, her voice firm.

"But I had my snowshoes all ready to go," Annalise teased.

Sarah narrowed her eyes and shook her head. "Nope. Not going to happen. No way. No how. If Ted wants to talk, he's going to have to come to me."

"Careful. You might regret that," Annalise warned, and the hairs on Sarah's arms rose.

CHAPTER 14

Sarah bolted upright in her bed.

"Wuz wrong?" Ashley asked, sleepily.

"It's nothing. Go back to sleep. I think someone is here."

"*What?*" Ashley was wide awake now, and sprang up to face Sarah.

"No one living. They're trying to connect. Go back to sleep," she repeated.

"You expect me to sleep now?" Ashley spat out, sotto voce.

"*Shhhh*…. I can't hear them with you talking."

Ashley laid back down and covered her head with the comforter.

"I can feel your presence, but I don't see you," Sarah spoke, barely above a whisper.

It was on the cusp of dawn and the light in the room was thin. She concentrated on a spot at the foot of their bed where she sensed the apparition. At first there was nothing, but then the figure of a man flitted in and out, not quite able to materialize fully. His mouth was moving, but the words were garbled and there were gaps between them.

En… later… turney… dill… Rachel

"I know you're speaking, but I can't hear you clearly."

Letter… enve… call… turney… dill… Rachel

"*Argh*," Sarah spat out the word in frustration as the spectral visage disappeared.

"Is it gone?" Ashley's muffled voice came from below the comforter.

"Yes," Sarah, said, her tone annoyed.

Ashley reappeared from under the covers.

"What did it want? And who was it?"

"I couldn't get all the words, but I did hear him say Rachel. I'm positive it had to be Ted Hartley."

"Who's he?"

"Our latest murder case."

CHAPTER 15

Eva shambled from her bedroom into the kitchen to find Reuben staring up at her beside his food dish.

It's about time you got up!

"Reuben, I'm up at the same time I get up every morning. I hardly think you're at risk of starving to death."

How could you sleep with all the commotion going on next door?

Eva looked at him with a perplexed expression on her face.

"What are you talking about?"

Look for yourself. There's been a police car parked in Rachel and Ted's driveway for the last two hours, and….

"Oh no, oh no, oh no."

Eva rushed to look out the dining room windows which faced the Hartley's house. A sheriff's patrol car was in the driveway, just as Reuben had said, and she recognized Deputy Carl Tremblay getting into the vehicle. Eva looked toward the door of the house and saw a haggard-looking Rachel waving goodbye and then closing the door.

"It's happened. I've got to tell Annalise."

What about my breakfast?

Reuben had followed her into the dining room and was wearing his annoyed expression.

"Alright, alright. I'll get your breakfast first." Eva's annoyed demeanor matched his. She retrieved a can from the pantry and scooped the contents into his bowl. "Do you think you can give me a minute now?" she growled, but he was already engrossed in devouring the food and ignored her.

Eva picked up her phone from its charging station and hit the button for Annalise, who answered on the second ring.

"It happened, didn't it?" Annalise greeted.

"I think so. Reuben let me know there was a police car at Rachel's house, and when I looked out the window, I saw Carl Tremblay pulling out of the driveway. Rachel was at the door, so she's okay, but I'm going to go check on her as soon as I get dressed. I just wanted to tell you that you were right. I can't think of any other reason why Carl would be there, and Reuben told me he'd been there for a couple hours before I got up."

"Thanks for calling. Let me know what she has to say. I have clients this morning, but I should be done by eleven." There was a pause. "Do you think we should have warned her?"

"Maybe. I don't know. At least she's okay. That's the main thing." Eva said reassuringly.

"You're right and it's too late now to dwell on the should haves, could haves."

"I'll call you after eleven."

Eva disconnected the call and hurried through her usual routine to catch Rachel before she left for work.

CHAPTER 16

"Rachel, I hope I'm not intruding, but I wanted to check on you. I saw the sheriff here earlier. Is something wrong?"

There were dark circles under her eyes and they had a distracted look. Finn was behind her and whined when he spotted Eva.

"I'm okay, but Ted's office was broken into. Come in out of the cold," she said, standing aside for Eva to enter. "We can talk in the living room. Finn woke me up at about three o'clock. He ran out of the bedroom and to the front door, barking all the way. I didn't want to open the door, so I peeked out the window and saw a car parked at the end of the driveway facing toward the street. A man was getting into the car or I would have thought he was just using the driveway to turn around. The only light was from the dome when he opened the door and he kept his headlights off when he drove away, so it was too dark to see who it was or what make or model he was driving. I waited a couple minutes just to make sure he was really gone and went out to Ted's office. I had this feeling that's why they were here and sure enough, it had been ransacked."

"Oh, my goodness. You must have been terrified. I'm so glad

the intruder only went to the office. Do you have any idea what they were looking for?"

"I have no idea. Ted didn't share a lot about his work with me. He said it was confidential, and it was better for me to not be involved. They took his laptop, but Ted kept the password encrypted, so even if it had anything on it, the thief would have to know how to crack the code to get into the files. Do you remember I told you I didn't think Ted's death was an accident?"

Eva nodded.

"I'm even more sure of it now. I think this break-in has something to do with it."

"Did you tell Carl your suspicions?"

"I was going to, but then I chickened out. I don't have any evidence to prove it, and I was afraid he'd think I was just an hysterical widow. Maybe this will get them to look deeper on their own if they make the connection. That's assuming they don't brush it off as just another break-in with the burglar looking for things they could sell."

"Will you be okay by yourself?"

"I have to go to work today. In fact, I should be getting ready now. Finn will keep me safe and I don't think the intruder will come back so soon, if at all. I just hope they got what they wanted. Deputy Tremblay told me he'd make sure they made extra checks on the house for the next few days."

"If you need anything, you let me know."

"I will, Eva. Thanks for being such a good neighbor and friend."

"You'd do the same for me. Have a good day at work."

CHAPTER 17

"We should call a special meeting so we can loop Jennifer and Sarah in on this," Annalise said after Eva had filled her in about the break-in.

"I agree. I'll send a group text. Can you be at my house at seven o'clock?"

"That works for me, but let's give Jen and Sarah a chance to weigh in. I can be flexible."

"Sounds good."

ANNALISE; JENNIFER; SARAH

> There's been a development with the Ted Hartley case. Can you meet at my house at 7?

JENNIFER

> Sure. We don't have anything going on tonight.

ANNALISE

> I'll be there.

SARAH

I have something important to tell you, too. See
you then.

Hmm, I wonder what that's about. Guess I'll find out.

"I'm going to do some sewing, Reuben. You're welcome to join me."

And how do you expect me to get my cat naps with all that sewing machine racket? Thanks, but I'll stay right here. Just look at that ray of sunshine coming in the window. I feel a nap coming on already.

He jumped up onto the ledge of the bay window, stretched out on his bed, and began to purr.

————

"Thank you all for coming on such short notice, but I didn't think it could wait. Annalise already knows this, but Ted's office was broken into last night. Rachel is safe, but the office was ransacked and his laptop was stolen."

"Your vision was true," Sarah said. It was a statement, not a question.

"I'm so relieved Rachel wasn't harmed. I never would have forgiven myself if she was."

"When I spoke with her, Rachel said she's even more convinced now that Ted's death wasn't an accident. I asked if she mentioned it to Carl Tremblay, but she hadn't because she was embarrassed to say anything without any proof."

"You tried to warn me to be careful of what I wished for, Annalise. I had a visit from Ted this morning," Sarah announced.

"You *what?*" Jennifer asked, her face mirroring the same shocked expression on Eva's and Annalise's faces.

"It was the first time that's happened around Ashley. She hid under the covers the whole time Ted was there." Sarah chuckled and the others joined in. "It wasn't a good connection, though. He was trying to tell me something, but it was like hitting a dead cell zone--no pun intended. The words were breaking up, so I only got little bits, and then he was gone."

"Did you understand any of it?" Eva asked.

"The only thing that was clear was the word Rachel. That's why I know it was Ted. I've never seen a picture of him, so wouldn't have recognized his face even if he wasn't fading in and out."

"Have you had a chance to do the background check on Henry Ward and Vinnie Barnes?" Jennifer asked.

"That's the other thing I wanted to tell you about. I haven't had time to do a deep dive, but Jim is right. Henry worked for Vinnie Barnes for about five years until this past September. He's gone out on his own, so that could be the reason he left. On the surface, it's not suspicious, but when I dug a little deeper, Vinnie's lifestyle doesn't match what he's showing as his business income. I haven't had time to do a full forensic accounting because it means I'll need to cover my tracks and my day job has been busy. My suspicion is that Henry caught on to what was going on and quit before he got wrapped up in any criminal activities."

"That matches with the meditation I did this afternoon," Annalise said. "It was after I'd spoken with you," she explained for Eva's benefit. "There must be some rift in the communication lines today, because it came to me in snippets rather than a complete picture. I saw hands exchanging money and there was a dark aura around one of them. That would fit with what you found out about Vinnie, Sarah."

"Where do we go from here? Do you think it's too soon to call Dennis and Phil? They helped us with Lily's case even though they weren't assigned to it," Jennifer asked.

There was a moment of silence as the others considered the option.

"It might not be a bad idea to get them in on it early," Sarah suggested.

"What about Rachel? Should we tell her anything?" Eva asked.

"That could go either way. It might help put her at ease to know we believe her, but it could be just as upsetting to know how we're helping," Jennifer reasoned.

"Okay. Do we need to draw straws to see who calls the detectives?" Eva asked.

Jennifer sighed. "I'm the one who got us into this, so I'll volunteer."

CHAPTER 18

hil's phone rang, and he picked up the receiver absent-mindedly as he continued reading the report he'd just finished. "Detective Roberts. May I help you?"

"Phil, it's Jennifer Ryder."

"Jennifer Ryder." His tone was friendly, and he put down the document to give her his full attention. "It's been a while since we last spoke. What can I... wait, you ladies aren't involved in another murder case, are you?" he asked warily, causing his partner, Dennis Smith, to look up from his paperwork with curiosity. He raised his eyebrows questioningly, but Phil held up his hand to let Dennis know he was listening to Jennifer.

"I wish I could say the call is purely social, but I wouldn't bother you if we didn't think it's a serious situation that's being overlooked as an accidental death."

Phil leaned his elbow on his desk and rested his forehead on the palm of his hand, anticipating what was coming. Dennis caught his attention by waving his hand and pointing to his phone, signaling he'd like to join the conversation.

"Dennis is here, too, Jen. He's going to join us."

"Oh, good. You both should hear this."

"Hi, Jen, what have you got for us?" Dennis asked.

Jennifer told them everything from the time she first experienced her vision while holding Ted's shirt until the events that the Club discussed the night before.

"If I didn't know all of you and you hadn't mentioned Vinnie Barnes, I might have told you the break-in probably had nothing to do with Ted Hartley's death and call it a day. Vinnie's not someone to cross, though. If he found out Ted was investigating him, I wouldn't put it past him to put something in motion to stop it. He might not have been the one to do it, but he has the connections to find someone who would," Phil said, when Jen was finished.

"We'll get a copy of the incident report and death certificate to see what else we can find out about what happened that day. We'll get back to you when we have more," Dennis promised.

They disconnected the call and Jennifer let out a long, slow breath.

"That was easier than I expected, Boscoe. The hard part is going to be letting Dave know what we're up to."

Woof!

Jennifer smiled as the dog laid his chin on her knee and she felt her shoulders relax.

"You're right. He'll understand."

———

"You're *what?*"

Boscoe was wrong. He doesn't understand. I was not expecting that reaction, Jennifer thought when she'd finished recounting the recent events about Ted Hartley to David.

"You know this won't be investigated if we don't get involved, Dave," she spoke quietly to bring down the temperature. "And Ted deserves closure. So does Rachel. Plus, we'll have Phil and Dennis working with us. They've always had our backs. They've never let us down or put us in danger."

"No, you've managed to do that all on your own." David was scowling, his hands were on his hips, and his mouth was set.

This isn't going well.

"It may not seem that way, but we really have been careful and the times when things got a little tense, it all worked out. Besides, we just need to give the evidence to them, and Phil and Dennis can take it from there. There's no reason we'd even have to get near Vinnie Barnes," she said with her fingers crossed behind her back, just in case.

"Promise me it will stay that way."

"I promise I'll do everything I can to keep it that way," she hedged.

David's face relaxed and his hands dropped to his side.

Jennifer took a deep breath through her nose as her body relaxed, too. *I hope you don't have to break that promise,* her inner voice cautioned.

CHAPTER 19

"Well, well, well, what do we have here, Max?"

Sarah was in her second-floor home office. It was a brilliant January day, with sunlight flooding the room, and when she looked out the window, she could see snow sparkling like diamonds in the park across the street in sharp contrast to the clump of evergreens at its border. Alternative rock music was playing quietly in the background.

Her golden retriever lifted his head, but not having any context to her question, laid it back down and closed his eyes.

"Don't worry, buddy, that was a rhetorical question," she smiled at her dog and returned her attention to her monitor. "Vinnie Barnes, you are not a nice man. I think you're setting Henry Ward up."

Max abruptly rose his head, the hair on his back stood up, and he began to growl as he stared at a spot near the doorway to the office. Sarah felt a chill in the air and immediately knew what was coming.

Good thing Ashley's at work, so she won't get freaked out again.

She turned toward the place where Max was looking and saw a shimmer waver and then slowly solidify. A tall man in his fifties was standing there dressed in hunting apparel.

"Ted?"

"Yes. Tell Rachel… call…"

His shape became more transparent, and Sarah sucked in her breath.

"No, no, don't go yet. *Concentrate*, Ted. Tell me the rest."

Seconds passed and she was afraid she was losing him again. She could see a faint impression of his face with his brows knit together and then, once again, his form was becoming more solid.

"Dylan Johnson has an envelope for Rachel. She needs to see what's inside. Explains everything."

His body shimmered, and then he was gone. The chill in the air disappeared. Max trotted over to Sarah, whining.

"It's okay, Max," she said, stroking his head to comfort him. "He's gone, and I don't think he'll be back. At least, not today. But how the heck am I going to tell Rachel she should call her attorney?"

She mulled over her dilemma for a solution when at last; it came to her. She had been instrumental in helping clear Dylan's name in October when he was falsely implicated in the death of his law partner. In the process, she'd had to reveal to him her ability to speak with the dead.

"I've got it, Max! I can just call Dylan."

Woof!

He licked her hand and returned to his bed, at ease now.

Sarah dialed the law firm's number.

"Mitchell & Johnson. How may I help you?" the assistant/receptionist announced.

"Amber, it's Sarah Pascal. Is Dylan available? I shouldn't take too much of his time."

"Let me check for you."

Elevator music filled the air space and then was interrupted by Dylan's voice.

"Sarah. Nice to hear from you, but it's a surprise. What can I do for you?"

"It's about Ted Hartley."

"Ted Hartley? How are you connected to him?" Dylan asked.

"*Welll*, it's a bit of a long story. Do you have a few minutes?"

She heard a soft whistle when she'd finished. She'd omitted the connection to Vinnie Barnes and Henry Ward… for now.

"So, do you still have an envelope that Ted asked you to hold for Rachel?"

"I'll need to check with Grace. She was doing the paperwork for Ted's estate. Let me get back to you."

Her phone rang ten minutes later and Sarah saw Grace Foster's name on the screen.

"Thanks for calling me back, Grace. I assume Dylan explained why I called."

"He gave me the salient facts, but I got the impression he was holding some things back."

Thank you, Dylan. What Grace doesn't know can't hurt her. Sarah knew Grace was hoping she would tell her what Dylan didn't, but remained quiet. *Grace is a smart woman. She'll catch on that I'm not going to tell her either.*

"So, you wanted to know about the envelope Ted gave us? I thought it was a little melodramatic at the time when he said we should give it to Rachel if anything happened to him. I could tell he was deadly serious, though, and the intention was to put it in his file for safekeeping. To be honest, it slipped my mind when I began probating his estate and it wasn't in the file, so out of sight, out of mind."

"Did someone else in the office give it to Rachel?"

"I asked Amber, but she hadn't given it to her either. It's possible it was misfiled, so I've asked her to look through our other files just in case. She's looking for it now."

"Thanks, Grace. Let me know one way or the other, please. I'm doing some research on an investigation he was working on and I think the information in that envelope could be linked to it." *Please don't ask me if Rachel hired me to do this, Grace. Just think that's why I'm involved. It's only a lie of omission… and Ted asked me, so really, I'm just doing what he asked,* Sarah rationalized.

"Of course. It might be a couple of days. We have a lot of files and Amber will have to fit it in with her other work."

"I understand. Thanks, Grace."

"Phew. I think we pulled that off, Max. Keep your fingers... well, your paws... crossed that Amber finds the file."

CHAPTER 20

"What should we start with tonight?" Eva asked.

"I'll go," Jennifer offered. "I talked to Phil and he's going to pull the incident report and death certificate and get back to me once they've had a chance to look them over. They warned me that Vinnie isn't someone to cross, so it didn't seem too far-fetched to him that Ted's accident might not have been an accident." She stopped to take a bite of her serving of chicken pot pie and moaned in delight. "Oh. My. Gosh. Annalise, this is amazing. Is it a family recipe?"

"It was my grandmother's. She made the lightest, flakiest crust. Mine doesn't even come close, but I suspect she was one of those cooks who left out some vital ingredient or technique when she shared her recipes. It couldn't possibly be my cooking." Annalise smiled and rolled her eyes. "I'm happy to give you a copy of the one she gave me, though."

"Me, too," Sarah said before putting another huge forkful in her mouth.

"Me, three. I've never had such a delicious pot pie," Eva added.

"I'll bring copies next week. To answer your original question, Eva, I had another vision about Ted's murder."

Sarah's fork stopped mid-way to her open mouth and looked at Annalise in surprise. Eva and Jennifer laid their forks on their plates and waited for her to continue.

"In this one, I saw a pair of hands that I'm sure were a man's. He was ratcheting bolts into the tree stand platform. He didn't completely tighten them and it looked very much like they had been partially cut so they would shear off when any weight was put on the platform. He was wearing a gold ring with a square cut ruby on his right hand. Men don't usually switch out rings like women do, so I think it's a ring he always wears. I know it's not anything that's helpful now, but maybe later it could be."

"That's good information, Lise. You never know when or how, but when the time is right, we'll know it. I talked to Phil about the case," Jennifer said.

"I might know a way," Sarah said, and all eyes turned to her.

After telling them about Ted's visit and her conversation with Dylan and Grace, she added, "We should tell them your vision, Annalise. It seems like Vinnie Barnes is on the police's radar and they'd know if he wears a ring like that. I was hoping to hear back from either Grace or Amber before coming tonight, but they must still be looking for the envelope."

"It's got to be Ted's case against Vinnie, don't you think? I bet he realized Vinnie might be onto him. I bet that's what the argument was about in Ted's office," Eva suggested.

"That makes sense to me. And it fits with something Grace said about Ted's behavior when he gave her the envelope, how serious he was. She didn't use these words, but she implied that it was like in the movies when they say it's in case of their untimely death."

"That pretty much seals the deal. I hope they find it soon," Annalise said.

"In the meantime, I'm still digging into Vinnie's and Henry's finances and business dealings," Sarah said.

"I'm so glad this is off my plate for now. Dave and I had a kerfuffle about it. He's worried I'll be in danger if I stay involved, but it sounds like the ball is in your court for now, Sarah," Jennifer said, the relief on her face evident.

"We've got your back, sister," Sarah said, smiling.

"That's what I tried to tell Dave. All of you, and Phil and Dennis. But if you need me, you let me know. I've got your backs, too," she said, looking into each of their faces and wiped at the corner of her eyes. "Now, before we get too mushy, how about some dessert? There's a white chocolate and raspberry cheesecake in the fridge with our names on it."

"You don't have to twist my arm. I'll get the plates and forks," Sarah said.

"Show and tell time, ladies. Let's see how your projects are coming along," Eva announced once dessert was finished, and the kitchen cleared of all the dinner debris.

"I'm making really good progress with Rachel's quilt, but I have a confession to make. I haven't been able to bring myself to use the chambray shirt, but I'm afraid Rachel will notice. I'm probably being silly because I doubt there's anything else I'd see if I held it again, but what should I do?" Jennifer asked.

"I could make the blocks with that shirt for you if you think it would help," Annalise offered. "My wall hanging isn't taking that long to do, so I've got extra time. I'll just need the instructions because I want to make sure I'm using the same technique for assembling it. Oh, and some of the background fabric."

"That would be awesome. Thank you, Lise."

"My pleasure," Annalise said, giving Jennifer a wink. She reached into her sewing tote and pulled out the wall hanging to show everyone.

"That is gorgeous! I love the way you've used the pinks and yellows for the sunset," Eva exclaimed.

"I'm thrilled with it, and I think my parents would have loved it."

"How could they not? You are such an artist, Annalise," Eva said. "I've been coming along with Meghan's throw. I think it's turning out nicely." Eva held it up for the others.

"And I've got the piecing done for Vivian's, so now it's on to the quilting. I'm thinking about doing it myself since it's a smaller size. It's about time I practiced more of the free-motion skills I learned in the class we took. It hasn't been a waste, though. I would never have found all of you if I hadn't taken the class. I love quilting, but I love you guys even more," Sarah said, her cheeks turning a faint shade of pink.

"Awww, I feel the same way. Group hug?" Eva suggested.

Here we go again. Aren't you ever going to stop with these kumbaya moments?

"No, Reuben, we aren't. The kumbaya moments make life worth living," Eva scolded.

"That reminds me, Sarah, once I get this quilt done, I'm going to Quilting Essentials to rent the long-arm machine to do mine. I haven't taken advantage of it since we took the class, but with a queen-size quilt, it would make my life so much easier than trying to do it at home," Jennifer said. "Have you considered taking yours there?"

"I hadn't, but I am now. Thanks for the reminder!" Sarah said.

"That's a great idea, Jen!" Eva said. "Before we call it a night, is there anything else we need to discuss about Ted's case?"

"Until we find out what's in that envelope or I can get concrete evidence against Vinnie, I think we're in a holding pattern," Sarah said.

"Well, maybe not," Eva said. "At some point, and I'm thinking it's better sooner than later, we're going to have to tell Rachel what we know. Once she gets the envelope, and it contains what we think it does, we could suggest she call Phil and Dennis. But how do we bring it up?"

The only sound in the room was the ticking of the wall clock.

At last Jen spoke, "It's going to have to come from you and me, Eva. She knows us and if we go together, it won't be as difficult for us... and her, I hope."

Eva sighed. "I already knew that was the way it would have

to go, but I was hoping someone else would come up with a better idea."

"Let's get together tomorrow and talk about the best way to approach her."

"If you decide you need us, we can be there, too, right, Sarah?" Annalise offered.

"I don't know how she'd feel when she hears her husband was in my bedroom, but of course. We're a team."

The sound of a cat coughing up a fur ball drew their eyes to Reuben. As soon as he knew they were paying attention, he gave them all a smug look and began licking his front paw.

Eva narrowed her eyes. "Let me guess. That was your way of saying you've had enough for one night."

Reuben stopped licking his paw, gave Eva a grin, and trotted out of the sewing studio and back to the living room.

"On that note, let's call it a night."

CHAPTER 21

"texted Rachel to ask her to meet us here when she gets home from work on the pretense of showing her the progress on the memory quilt. I told her we thought it would be easier to do it at my place instead of yours because I'm right next door. She said she's usually home by four." Eva informed Jennifer on the phone the following morning.

"Good thinking. I'll come by at three thirty so we can go over one more time how we're going to break this news. See you then."

"Oh, shoot," Eva juggled the phone as it rang at the same time she was disconnecting her call with Jen. "Sarah, hi," she said, once she gained control of the device.

"You're not going to believe this. Well, probably you will. Anyway, sorry I'm babbling, but I'm just so excited," Sarah blurted out.

Eva smiled as she waited patiently for her to continue.

"Grace just called. Amber found the envelope! It was misfiled, but they got in touch with Rachel and she's stopping by on her way home this afternoon to pick it up. Of course, she couldn't tell me what's inside even if it wasn't for the confidentiality issue because they don't know either. Ted's instructions were that Rachel open it."

"That's fantastic! This could be a major breakthrough. You're sure you're still okay with Jen and I telling her about Ted's visit?"

"I think it could help her believe we're for real if it has the information we suspect it does. How else would we have known about it if it wasn't for Ted telling me?" Sarah said.

"Keep your fingers crossed that it works. But even if she doesn't believe us, we can tell her to take it to Phil and Dennis and they can take it from there. We can still help them if they need it, even without Rachel knowing we're involved."

"Good luck! Let me know how it goes."

"Will do."

———

"I'm so nervous, I can hardly sit still," Jennifer confessed to Eva while they waited for Rachel to arrive. "Do you think this is really the way we should do this?"

"Honestly, I'm not sure, but we have to try."

Rachel is here, Reuben announced.

"Deep breath. It's now or never," Eva said. "You stay here and I'll get the door."

"Have I kept you waiting?" Rachel asked, as she took off her coat and handed it to Eva, who was waiting to hang it in the closet. "Hi, Jen, I'm so excited to see what you've got done on the quilt."

I hope you'll still feel that way after we tell you the real reason we asked you to come, Jennifer thought, but put on a warm smile for Rachel's benefit.

"We were just sitting here yakking. Let's sit and chat for a few minutes and then Jen can show you the quilt," Eva said and waited until Rachel was settled before continuing. "You've known me a long time and I hope you trust me and don't think any of my screws are loose," she began.

The corners of Rachel's mouth turned up in a half-smile, but she tilted her head and scrunched up her eyebrows questioningly. *Where's she going with this?* she thought.

Eva glanced at Jennifer, who nodded her head encouragingly.

"When we first started our quilting club, we discovered a secret each of us had been hiding from the time we were little. We all have a gift most people don't, and we've used our abilities to help solve murders. You've told me you have a feeling Ted's death wasn't an accident and we believe you."

Jen took over with their confession.

"My gift is psychometry and when I held Ted's blue chambray shirt, I had a vision of the day he died and how it happened. I haven't said anything before because I was afraid it would upset you and we didn't have any proof that what I said was true, so we couldn't go to the police. There was someone else there that day and we think it was Vinnie Barnes and he is the one responsible for Ted's death. He sabotaged the platform, so it gave way when Ted stepped onto it."

By now, Rachel's eyes were wide as saucers and her mouth gaped slightly.

Eva took over from Jennifer to reveal more of what the club had discovered.

"I can understand what animals are saying. Finn told me that Vinnie Barnes didn't come just to cancel the hunting trip. He learned that Ted had been hired to investigate him and he was warning Ted if he didn't back off, he would pay. Finn was there in the office when this happened. This may be the hardest part for you to accept, but another club member, Sarah Pascal, can communicate with the dead. Ted came to her and told her he had given Dylan Johnson an envelope, which was supposed to be delivered to you upon his death."

Rachel gasped.

"The reason I was running late was because Dylan's office

called me this morning to tell me they'd found an envelope Ted left for me. It had been misfiled or they would have given it to me right after he died. I have it in my purse, but I haven't opened it yet because I came straight here from their office and, to be honest, I'm almost afraid to."

"We think it contains the evidence Ted had gathered against Vinnie, and we think Henry Ward is the person who hired him," Jennifer said.

"Would you be willing to open it now?" Eva asked.

Rachel sat in stunned silence for a moment before picking up her purse to retrieve the envelope. Her hands were shaking as she unsealed the large manilla envelope and removed the contents. Her eyes filled with tears when she saw the paper on top of the pile of documents.

"It's a letter from Ted," she explained. She read the letter and then looked up at Eva and Jennifer. "He said exactly what you've told me. Henry Ward hired him because Vinnie was blackmailing him. The rest of these papers are the proof that Vinnie is laundering money through his construction business."

"This has to be what the intruder was trying to find," Eva said.

"What should I do now?" Rachel asked.

"We've worked with two homicide detectives who know what we do and we trust each other. I've already told them some of what we've learned and they said they'd be willing to help, and now that you have this file, it will make it easier for them to make the case official instead of off the books. I can call them right now, if you're okay with that," Jennifer offered.

Rachel nodded. "Yes, I am. Please call them."

CHAPTER 22

Jennifer pulled her phone out of her purse and searched the Contacts for Phil's number. The line rang twice before he picked up. "Phil, it's Jennifer Ryder, and I have Eva and Rachel Hartley, Ted Hartley's widow, here with me. I've got you on speaker. We have something we want to share with you."

"I'm all ears."

"Dylan Johnson is Rachel's attorney and today they gave her an envelope from Ted that contains the evidence he discovered from his investigation into Vinnie Barnes. We think you and Dennis should have the file so you can reopen the case as a murder instead of an accident."

"Since we talked, Dennis and I pulled the report for Mr. Hartley's case. It was ruled an accident and no foul play was suspected, so there wasn't a more thorough investigation performed."

"I didn't see what happened prior to Ted falling from the platform in my vision. After the man who was there—and I can't say for sure it was Vinnie Barnes—checked to see that Ted wasn't alive, he walked back out the way he came in and covered up his tracks."

"Mrs. Hartley, it says that you notified the police when your husband didn't return home that evening, but they didn't start searching until the next day. Is that correct?"

"Yes. I have an app on my phone that tracks… tracked… Ted's location on his phone. I gave them the coordinates, and that's how they were able to find him sooner. I'd made Ted agree that I could do that in case there was ever trouble because of his job taking him places that could put him in danger and especially whenever he was hunting. I wanted them to search for him when I called, but by then it was dark and they said he could have just dropped his phone somewhere and was already on his way home. They told me to call back in the morning if he still hadn't come back. I know now it wouldn't have made any difference, but I was so frustrated and angry at the time." Rachel's mouth was set and her hands were clasped tightly in her lap.

"I'm sorry you had to go through that," Phil said in a calm, sincere tone of voice.

"Thank you."

Eva's face lit up. "Jen, we almost forgot! Phil, do you have anything in your reports about Vinnie Barnes wearing a ring? Annalise had a vision in which she saw someone changing money with another person. It was just two pairs of hands, no faces, but she thinks it's connected to this case. And then later she had another vision in which a man was tampering with the bolts on the platform. She only saw the hands this time, too, but on his right hand, the man was wearing a gold ring set with a square cut ruby."

"I'd have to check about the ring. There's no mention of the bolts that attached the platform to the tree, so we assume no one bothered to look for them to examine for signs of tampering. There was snow on the ground, so if they fell out, they could have been buried under the snow. Or it could mean whoever tampered with the bolts took them with them," Dennis said.

"You know the drill, ladies. This isn't enough for Dennis and me to reopen the investigation until we have the paperwork Ted gave you, Mrs. Hartley. Would you be able to bring it to us tomorrow?"

"Yes, I could do that on my lunch break, but I'll need to know where."

They exchanged contact information and disconnected the call.

"How are you doing?" Jennifer asked.

"I'm a little shell-shocked," Rachel admitted. "There's a part of me that isn't accepting what you've told me about all of your abilities. But there are too many details that you couldn't have known about otherwise, so I guess I have to at least give you the benefit of the doubt. I'm going to need some time to process it all."

"I just hope it hasn't affected how you feel about us, Rachel. That's always our biggest fear whenever we tell anyone about ourselves and why we only do it on a need-to-know basis." Eva's expression was earnest as she searched Rachel's face for any sign this was happening.

"I'm going to have to process that, too," Rachel said. "But I've known you both for years, and you've never been anything other than kind, salt of the earth people. I can't imagine you ever trying to scam someone, so even though I've never believed paranormal abilities are real, I might have to rethink that," she said, smiling.

Jennifer's and Eva's shoulders relaxed, and they smiled at Rachel.

"You have no idea how worried we've been about telling you this. In the end, we knew we didn't have any choice. It was more important that Ted's murderer be brought to justice. I'm just so glad you're willing to keep an open mind," Jennifer said.

"I can only imagine how you must have been struggling with it. How do other people react when you tell them?"

Eva and Jennifer exchanged glances and broke into wide grins.

"Pretty much the same as you did," Eva told her, but then her expression became serious. "We have a request to make that we hope you will honor. Please don't share this with anyone else. I'm sure you can figure out why we want to keep it a secret."

"Of course. I've only lived in Glen Lake for five years, but it's not the first small town Ted and I lived in, so I get it. I'm just so thankful you took the risk. It's been weighing on me ever since he died that it wasn't an accident, but now I don't feel so alone. It's like I can breathe again knowing that someone believes me," she said, and dabbed her fingers at the corner of her right eye.

"Group hug?" Eva asked, rising from her chair and walking toward Rachel, with Jennifer following her lead.

Eva spied Reuben over Rachel's shoulder as he trotted into the living room from where he'd been sleeping on Eva's bed and stopped dead in his tracks.

Meow, he uttered disgustedly when he spotted the three women embracing, and turned on his heels to return to her bedroom.

CHAPTER 23

ettle down, Rachel admonished the butterflies in her stomach when she arrived at the police station with Ted's file. She sat with her hands folded protectively over the envelope in her lap while she waited in the reception area for one of the detectives to meet her. It wasn't long before a forty-something-year-old man pushed open the door from the inner offices and entered the room. *I think I can trust him,* she thought, taking in his warm smile and serious blue eyes as they met hers.

"Thank you for coming, Mrs. Hartley," Phil Roberts greeted her.

Rachel stood and shook his proffered hand. "Thank you for seeing me."

"I know you're on your lunch break, so we'll try to make this quick. My partner, Dennis Smith, is waiting for us in the conference room. Follow me."

He led her down a hallway with rooms on both sides. Rachel peeked in as they passed. *These must be rooms for interviews.* Each had a small table with four chairs, two on either side. She was so focused on looking into them that she nearly bumped into Phil's back when he stopped and stood aside to usher her into the room where another man was sitting. Dennis was about the same age as Phil, but slightly taller and had thinning brown hair. He rose from his chair when she entered the room.

"Mrs. Hartley, I'm Detective Dennis Smith," he said, also extending his hand for her to shake. "Please have a seat."

Both men waited for her to settle into her chair before sitting opposite her. She laid the envelope on the table and slid it toward them.

"Jennifer Ryder and Sarah Pascal have told me a little of what they've learned about your husband's death," Phil began.

Rachel frowned at the mention of the name Sarah Pascal. She still wasn't sure if she was comfortable with the idea that Ted was in another woman's bedroom, even if it was in his ghost form. Detective Roberts was still talking, bringing her attention back to the room.

"We can't reopen the case on our own, but we think with more information tying your husband's investigation into Vinnie Barnes, we can take it to our supervisor. Have you looked through the file he left for you?"

"Yes. Ted was hired by a man by the name of Henry Ward. He didn't know how, but he was convinced that Vinnie Barnes found out about his investigation and that's why he gave all of this to Dylan Johnson in case something happened to him." Rachel blinked away the tears filling her eyes and bit her lip to keep her composure. "I made a copy of everything and put it in the wall safe in Ted's office last night. The intruder must not have known about it, because it wasn't disturbed during the break-in. It's hidden behind a picture, so it's not obvious unless you know where to look. Although it wouldn't have mattered because the safe was empty at the time of the break-in."

"We've read the report about the burglary at your husband's office, but since we don't know who the perpetrator was, we can only assume it's connected to Mr. Barnes," Dennis picked up the conversation. "We'll keep this under the radar as much as possible. The last thing we want, both for the case and for your safety, is to tip him off."

"Of course. I appreciate that," Rachel replied. She glanced at her watch. "I have to leave now or I'll be late. Unless there's anything else?"

"This should do it for now, but we have your number if we need to get in touch. I'll take you back to the reception area," Phil said, standing. Dennis followed suit and picked up the envelope, but remained behind.

After seeing Rachel off, Phil returned to their office. Dennis had emptied the envelope onto his desk and was reading through the papers.

"What do you think?" Phil asked.

"This corroborates some of what Sarah has already told us." He sighed. "I'm not sure it's going to be enough to rule his death as a homicide, though. He put together a strong case against Barnes threatening Henry Ward and blackmailing him to stay quiet about his money laundering. It's all stuff you'd expect a PI to have about someone he's investigating. There's nothing that hints that Vinnie threatened Ted directly, which would make him feel his life was in danger. Heck, they were even supposed to be going deer hunting together. On the surface, it sounds more like they were friends than enemies. We must be missing something." Dennis looked glum.

"Our hands may be tied until we get the boss's okay, but we need to bring Henry Ward in."

"Or maybe we don't tell the boss," Dennis said, grinning.

CHAPTER 24

his isn't making sense. Sarah scowled at her computer monitor and sat back in her chair as she read the information she'd discovered one more time. *What's the connection?* Her eyes went from one file to another, trying to make sense of it, and then the light went on in her brain. She sprang forward in her chair so forcefully it rolled back a couple of inches. Max leaped up onto all fours from his bed where he'd been sleeping and his head swiveled around the room to see what had prompted her sudden action.

"Sorry, buddy. I didn't mean to scare you," Sarah said, chuckling, and then stroked the dog's head to reassure him. "I think I just figured out something new that will help the case."

She picked up her phone to inform the detectives of her find.

"Dennis, it's Sarah Pascal. I think I may have found a clue tying Vinnie Barnes to Ted Hartley but I wanted to ask if Ted already put this in the envelope for Rachel. I think it would be a good idea for us to compare notes. Can you and Dennis bring his information to my house?"

"We were just going to call to ask you the same thing! Is this a good time for you? We could be there in fifteen minutes."

"That would be perfect. See you soon."

———

"Come on up to my office," Sarah said, leading the way.

Phil chuckled. "I can hear Max. How did you manage to get by him first?"

"I had to sneak out before you got here so I could close the door without waking him up. He's very excited to see you," she said, chuckling.

They could all hear Max's whines and the scratching on Sarah's office door as they ascended the stairs.

"Whoa, Max," Sarah said as soon as she opened the door and was pushed aside by the eager dog rushing his way past her to greet the detectives. His tail wagged enthusiastically and he pranced in front of them as he sought out their hands to lick, making both of the men chuckle. They each bent down to stroke his head and back before entering the room with Max following closely behind.

"Okay, you've said hello. Lay down now. The detectives and I have some business to discuss."

Max looked at her forlornly. He gave her his best puppy dog eyes, but her stern look let him know it wouldn't work and his tail stilled. He walked to his bed and plopped down, resting his chin on his paws but faced his human and her friends to take advantage of any sign he was welcome again.

"Why don't we start with Ted's envelope?" Sarah suggested. "Hopefully, I haven't wasted your time bringing you here if we already have the same information."

Phil handed her the envelope and she slid the contents onto her desk. The detectives sat silently while she read through the paperwork.

"Oh, good, it isn't a total waste of your time. I had most of what's in here, but this morning I found a new shell corporation that I've been able to trace back to Vinnie Barnes. It was registered a few days before Ted died so I don't think he'd had time to find it himself. On the surface, it seems banal enough. Just your typical set up to launder money but there were only two payouts and then it was closed. It was to an offshore account and the first payment was the day before Ted's murder. The second was the day after his body was found. I don't think Vinnie Barnes killed Ted. I think this was a murder for hire."

CHAPTER 25

"Do you know who the hit man is?" Dennis asked.

"Not yet, but I'm confident enough that's what happened that I didn't want you to waste time following the wrong lead."

"But you think Vinnie is the one who hired him?" Phil asked.

"That part I am sure of. His name is on the paperwork for the shell corporation. I had to dig down to find it, but it's there, and I can tie it back to another of his accounts as the source of the funding. I'm going to keep looking to get the identity of the account holder for the offshore account. What I also haven't figured out yet is how Vinnie realized Ted was onto him. Have you had a chance to talk to Henry Ward?"

"Not yet. It's not an official case so we've been making sure to keep everything under wraps. His office told us he was taking a vacation and won't be back for another week."

"That also means we can't use any of this information since you didn't go through proper channels. It wouldn't hold up in court," Dennis said. His shoulders were slumped and Sarah saw the disappointment on his face.

"I might be able to find a way around that," Sarah said, smiling and winked at him. "But first, we have to get the case opened as a murder or at least a suspicious, not accidental, death."

"We need to find those bolts and to question Henry Ward. Are you up for a walk in the woods?" Phil asked Dennis.

Dennis raised his hand to his forehead and his head sank to his chest as he let out his breath in a huff. "I was afraid you were going to suggest that."

CHAPTER 26

"I think we should take what we've got to the chief and tell him what we'd like to do," Dennis said once they were in their car. "If we go out to the deer stand, we need to have a crime scene tech with us so we can keep this by the book. We could go out there on our own, but how would we explain why we were there in the first place?"

Phil nodded, keeping his eyes on the road while he drove. "I see your point. Do you think he'll go for it?"

"I figure we've got a fifty-fifty shot at it. Everyone knows Vinnie Barnes is dirty and Ted Hartley's file makes a good case that he was blackmailing Henry Ward. It's still a stretch from that to proving Ted's death was foul play and he's responsible, but it might get us in the door based on the circumstantial evidence."

"And you're thinking if we have the proof the tree stand was sabotaged, it could help us when we interview Henry Ward?" Phil asked.

"I hadn't, but now that you mention it, that's exactly what I was thinking," Dennis said, with a big grin on his face.

Phil gave him a side-eye, but smiled. They'd been partners for several years and knew how they each thought.

———

"I can't believe we pulled that off," Phil said when they were back in their office.

"Me either, but I'm glad we got the chief's blessing. I'll call Ian Nelson and set up a time to go out to the deer stand. Cross your fingers we can do it this week while we're having a January thaw so there shouldn't be much snow on the ground."

"And cross your toes, too, that whoever sabotaged the platform didn't take the bolts with them," Phil replied.

CHAPTER 27

"'ve been dying to hear how it went with Rachel," Annalise practically pounced on Eva and Jennifer at their next meeting.

"It went much better than I was expecting. Wouldn't you agree, Jennifer?" Eva asked.

Jennifer nodded her head and relief was written all over her face. "I do. But, honestly, I think a part of me knew that she would trust us enough to believe we weren't pulling her leg or playing some cruel joke on her."

"Phil and Dennis came to see me and they're going to be the ones tromping out in the woods," Sarah informed them, leaning forward to take a cracker and scoop it into the spinach artichoke dip. "Mmm, I love this stuff," she said, holding her other hand below her chin to make sure none slid onto the table before it made it into her mouth. She munched contentedly and immediately reached for another one.

"That must mean that the paperwork Rachel took to them was important enough to start an official investigation," Eva said, waiting her turn for the dip.

"And I found a clue." Sarah filled them in on the shell corporation and her meeting with the detectives.

"I'm starting to feel optimistic this is going to get solved and Ted will have justice," Jennifer said, dipping her cracker in the dip just as Sarah was about to take another. "Save some room for dinner, girl," she teased.

"You don't really think a few crackers and dip are going to ruin my appetite, do you?" Sarah asked, smiling. "I've got the metabolism of a hummingbird."

Eva sighed. "I remember those days. And then in my late forties, one day I woke up and my hummingbird had turned into a sloth. Enjoy it while you can."

"I'll have one for you. The calories are on me," Sarah said, winking at her.

"How are everyone's projects coming along?" Eva asked to take the conversation away from food.

"I'm making good progress with mine. I don't always cut everything out before I begin sewing, but this pattern worked really well for that. Once that was done, I've been stitching the blocks production style so I don't have to stop as often to trim them and square them up."

"I don't think I would have made a Carolina Lily quilt on my own, but it's been a fun project. I'm glad you chose that, Sarah," Eva said.

"It's been fun for me, too. Although sometimes I get sad when I think about the times I saw Lily wearing the clothes we're using."

"Do you think there will be enough left over to make yourself a memory quilt? Or maybe even a pillow," Annalise suggested.

"Well, duh. Why didn't I think of that? I love that idea, Annalise. Thanks!" Sarah said. "And someday I'd like to get together with you so you can show me how you do your art quilts."

"That's a great idea. Why don't we use one of our meetings so you can teach all of us, Lise?" Jennifer asked.

"I second that," Eva added.

"In that case, how can I say no?" Annalise asked, smiling at
the others.

CHAPTER 28

"I read the report and this was ruled accidental. So, what are you guys hoping to find?" Ian Nelson asked the detectives.

The three men, their jackets unzipped and wearing boots despite the lack of snow on the ground, were standing in the clearing facing the stand which still dangled vertically from the tree, held up by the remaining set of bolts. The sky was a cloudless, brilliant blue and the temperature a comfortable forty degrees. It was one of those rare January days that gave Mainers a respite from the freezing winter conditions.

"Ted Hartley left a file with his attorney with information he'd gathered while investigating Vinnie Barnes with instructions to deliver it to his widow. He was hired by Henry Ward who was—maybe still is—being blackmailed by Vinnie. We think the tree stand might have been tampered with if Vinnie found out Ted was investigating him, but we need proof to officially reopen the case," Phil said.

"Okay," Ian said, gazing up at the platform. "Logic says we should be looking for the bolts that gave way. I don't remember anything in the report about them being retrieved at the time."

He opened his field kit and took out a small metal detector.

"You picked a good time to do this. A week ago, the ground

would have been covered in snow. The detector could have still picked them up, but they should be easier to spot."

The two detectives stood off to the side while Ian moved the metal detector back and forth over the ground's surface. At first, the silence was broken only by the chirping of chickadees in the nearby trees. Their slouched shoulders reflected their pessimism that the bolts were still there, but then the distinctive beeping sound alerting them to the discovery of something metallic brought them to attention. Ian ran the detector across a pile of sodden, brown leaves and was rewarded with more beeps. Taking an evidence bag from his kit and donning a pair of nitrile gloves, he brushed away the leaves.

"I've got one and it's broken in half," he announced, and removed a plastic placard with the number one printed on it and placed it next to the bolt pieces. He then took a photograph to document the find before placing them in the bag and into his field kit. He swept away more leaves with no luck before moving over another foot and ran the detector over the ground again. This time, the beeping sounded and under the pile, he discovered the second bolt, also in pieces. He repeated the process of documenting the bolt and deposited those fragments in a separate evidence bag.

After not finding any more bolts after a few more minutes of searching, he looked up at the platform and the ladder leading to it.

"There's probably not any others, but I should go up to see how the other side was connected before we go and see if there are any obvious signs of tampering," he told the detectives who nodded their understanding.

Ian ascended the ladder and examined the deer stand for several minutes before descending again and walking to his kit. Crouching down with his back to Phil and Dennis, he removed the bolts from the bag and inspected them closely on all sides before finally turning and addressing the detectives.

"They're a little rusty, but from what I can see, the bolts were cut partway through. I'll need to get them back to the lab to make it official, but I think you've got a case of foul play here."

Dennis let out his breath. "That's great news. I know it's not something we can hang on Vinnie, but if it will get the case reopened, we can take it from there."

"That's all I can do here today. I'll send you my report as soon as it's ready. In a couple days," he said, answering the question Phil was about to ask.

The sound of a branch cracking and rustling leaves made them all jump.

Three heads swiveled in the direction of the noise and they stood completely still.

What the heck was that? Dennis thought and his pulse raced as the adrenaline kicked in.

"It's just a deer," Phil said under his breath, making Dennis wonder if he'd meant to say it out loud. Phil pointed toward a gap in the trees.

Ian and Dennis's shoulders relaxed as they spotted the doe he was pointing out at the same time she spotted them. The deer turned and ran, her white tail the last they saw of her.

"Let's get out of here. This place is making me jumpy," Dennis said.

"You won't get any argument from me," Ian replied and led the way back through the woods.

CHAPTER 29

Sarah was focused on her monitor as she followed another lead for the shell corporation she was sure had been set up by Vinnie to pay the hit man who killed Ted.

Ding!

"Not now," she said aloud to the text message notification, and continued her search.

Ding!

"Alright, alright," she grumbled and clicked on the messaging app.

"Looks like another spammer, Max," she said when she didn't recognize the number and was about to delete it when another *ding* announced a follow-up text and in all capital letters she read

STOP WHAT YOU'RE DOING OR YOU'LL
BE NEXT

Sarah sucked in her breath as she shot upright in her chair and goosebumps broke out on her arms. She sat staring at the screen, too stunned to move until anger replaced her surprise.

"Not going to happen, whoever you are. I'm too close now,"

she said, her face set with determination. "I'm just going to have to be more sneaky. Right, Max?"

Max jumped up from his bed and trotted to Sarah's side, giving her hand a lick in solidarity.

CHAPTER 30

At the same time as Sarah was receiving the text, Rachel was leaving school for the day.

Her eyebrows scrunched together when she spotted the piece of paper stuck under her windshield wiper. She looked around at the other cars in the lot thinking it might be a flyer that everyone had received, but hers was the only one. She pulled up the wiper blade to remove the note that was folded in half and tucked underneath.

"Oh, no!" she gasped as her hand flew to her mouth and she looked from side to side and then turned in a circle to see if anyone was nearby.

Typed on the paper were the words

WE'RE WATCHING YOU. DON'T END UP LIKE YOUR HUSBAND.

Rachel stuffed the note into her pocket and fumbled at the door handle, giving silent thanks that she didn't need to use a key to unlock it. She slid into the car and slammed the door shut, locking it as soon as it was closed. Her hands were trembling as she pressed the ignition button.

You need to settle yourself before you start moving, she thought, fighting the impulse to leave the parking lot as quickly as possible. *Take a few deep breaths.* She shut her eyes and took several breaths until at last, her shoulders relaxed and her fingers unclenched in her lap. Taking a last look around, but seeing no one, she put the car in Drive and slowly pulled out of the lot and headed home.

CHAPTER 31

"Jennifer, it's Rachel Hartley. I think we need to stop investigating Ted's accident."

"Rachel, what's wrong? You sound upset."

"I think this investigation could be putting us in danger. I couldn't live with myself if something happened to anyone else."

"What's changed your mind?"

"I found a note on my windshield when I was leaving school. It said… I was being watched… and warned me I could end up like my husband," Rachel said, her voice hitching as she fought back tears.

"*What?*" Jennifer's eyes widened with surprise. "Did you keep the note? You should give it to Phil and Dennis. They need to know about this."

Jennifer felt David's eyes on her but avoided looking at him. They were in their kitchen prepping their dinner and Jennifer turned her back to him.

"I don't know. Maybe I should just drop it. It's bad enough that Ted has died because of this. If I tell them to stop investigating, no one else needs to get hurt."

"I can't force you to tell them, but there's no guarantee

whoever is behind this will just let it go. If they're put in jail, they can't hurt anyone else. And Phil and Dennis are already working on it and making some headway. Do you trust them?"

Rachel hesitated. "I think so. They seemed like they believed me and wanted to help."

"I've known them for a while now and I would trust them with my life. If nothing else, just give them the note and let them do their jobs. There shouldn't be any reason for you to be more involved."

"I guess you're right. I'll call them and tell them what happened."

"And Rachel, you're not alone. You have Eva next door and Annalise and I are here in Glen Lake if you ever need to reach out, even if it's just to hear a friendly voice."

"Thanks, Jen. You're a good friend."

"It's what friends do. Let me know how it goes with Phil and Dennis."

"I will."

"What was that about?" David asked when Jennifer disconnected the call.

Jennifer turned to face him and braced herself mentally before replying. *This could get ugly if I don't stay calm.* She hadn't technically broken her promise to him about not getting more involved, but she wasn't going to let a friend down either.

"Rachel Hartley found a threatening note on her windshield when she was leaving school today. It said she was being watched and could be next."

David scowled at her. "I told you this could get dangerous."

"And you heard me tell her to take it to Phil and Dennis to let them handle it," she said, her voice testy.

David's scowl softened. "I did, but I'm still worried."

"I know," Jennifer replied, her tone gentler now. "Sarah is the one who's been doing most of the investigating on this and I really have been keeping myself out of it." *So far.* "I haven't been involved since I introduced Rachel to Phil and Dennis.

This was the first time since then that I've heard anything more about it."

"Then why did Rachel call you?"

"My guess is it's because I encouraged her to go to them and ask them to reopen the case after she got the envelope Ted left her."

David nodded his head. "Okay, that makes sense. And you don't think anyone would connect you to the case?"

Jennifer considered the possibility.

"I don't see how they would. If you think you need to be worried about someone, it's more likely to be Sarah than me."

I should call her to tell her about Rachel. But I'd better wait until after dinner so I can have more privacy.

David wrapped her in his arms and kissed the top of her head.

"I'm sorry if I came across too strong. It's only because I'm worried about your safety. I love you."

Jennifer rested her head on his chest, feeling safe in the comfort of his embrace. "I know. I love you, too."

———

Jennifer maintained a calm exterior but inside her impatience to get dinner over so she could reach out to Sarah was reaching its limit. Once the kitchen was clean, though, she grabbed her cell, deciding to text instead of call.

"I'm going downstairs for a bit to work on the quilt for Rachel. I won't be too long," she told David and pocketed her phone.

Thought you should know that Rachel had a note on her car threatening her.

I got one, too. On my phone. Will tell you about it at tomorrow's meeting.

Jennifer's eyebrows shot up when she read the message. Her patience was getting a workout tonight if she'd have to wait for Sarah's news, too.

Can't wait to hear the deets. See you tomorrow.

CHAPTER 32

"Do you want to start or should I?" Jennifer asked Sarah when they were all gathered for their potluck supper/club meeting.

"I'll go. Yesterday I was digging into the shell corporation I think was used to pay whoever tampered with the deer stand, when I got a text warning me to back off or I'd be next."

Eva and Annalise both gasped.

"I got in touch with Phil and Dennis to tell them. While we were talking, they got the report from the crime scene evidence technician. The good news is that he confirmed the bolts were cut so they would shear off when weight was put on the platform. The bad news is that there's no way to conclusively tie them to Vinnie Barnes. That type of bolt is something his construction company would have on hand just as a normal part of his business. More good news is it should be enough to reopen Ted's case so they can investigate deeper."

"What about you? That text sounds too close to home. You and Ashley could be in danger," Eva cautioned.

"I'm not giving up, but I am being more careful. I think I must have triggered an alert when I started poking into the account even though I thought I'd shielded myself. The guys are going to talk to Danielle Larson at the DA's office about what I've collected."

"Is she the one who helped with Lily Sullivan's case?" Jennifer asked.

"Yes, that's her. I might have to stretch the truth a bit to explain how I've gotten the information I have so far, but we have a history, so I'm not too concerned about it. If nothing else, it should speed up what they'll need to do to track down the digital trail and figure out who the hit man was."

Jennifer stepped in when Sarah had finished.

"Yesterday Rachel got a threat, too, that someone put on her windshield. She called me last night and wanted to drop the investigation but I convinced her to turn the note over to Phil and Dennis and let them handle it. Dave wasn't very happy with me at first. He thought I was still too involved, but I finally got him calmed down. I'm hoping the detectives can find a way to check on Rachel, especially while she's at work. She has Finn to protect her at home and you, Eva, but I'd feel so much better if I knew there were patrol cars checking, too."

"I'll be on the lookout for any suspicious vehicles," Eva reassured her.

"I might have something to add although it's not anything that can hold up in court," Annalise began. "When I was sewing the blocks with the fabric from Ted's shirt… I brought those with me tonight, by the way, Jen… I had a vision that clarified the one I had before about the ring. At first, I thought it must be Vinnie Barnes's hands and ring that I was seeing, but now my intuition is telling me it had to be those of the hit man. And this time I saw more of him, but only from the back. He has dark hair, maybe brown, but I think it's black. In the vision, it was long and tied back in a ponytail. I know that won't help if he's cut it since then, but I found pictures of Vinnie online and his hair is gray."

The ladies sat quietly to process the information they'd just shared.

"Well, that was a lot to take in," Eva said. "Are we ready to talk about quilts?"

"I'll be right back. The blocks I did with Ted's shirt are in my sewing tote," Annalise said.

"We'll wait until you get back," Eva said.

"Here you go," Annalise said when she returned, and held them out for Jennifer.

Jennifer reached her hand out tentatively to take them from her. She exhaled audibly when she touched the fabric and no visions overtook her.

"I admit I was afraid to hold them, but the shirt must have served its purpose because there's nothing there now. They came out beautifully, Annalise. I've got all the others done so I can put them together and with a little luck, I should have the top finished tonight. I made an appointment with Evelyn to rent the longarm machine at the end of next week, so I'm on a deadline."

"That's terrific, Jen. Do you already have the layout figured out?"

"I think so, but I might need to use your quilt design wall just to make sure before I start sewing. Ripping out seams is not high on my list of things to do when I'm quilting."

"Of course! It's folded up in a corner, but it's not a problem to take it out," Eva said.

"Mine is almost finished, too. That reminds me that I need to call Evelyn about making an appointment, but I might just take it in for Nicki to do it instead. I've been focusing my spare time on Ted Hartley's case."

"I'm nearly done with the one for Meghan, but I'm planning to do the quilting on my little longarm machine. It's just a throw size so will be a good fit for that. The top is all pieced so I'm going to use tonight's time to make the sandwich. It should be done by next week's meeting," Eva said.

"I can't thank you enough for helping me out with that. Meghan is going to be so excited to see it finished. I've given her some hints but not so many it will ruin the surprise. That reminds me, I was thinking that we could invite Rachel, Vivian, and Meghan to come to a meeting so we could give them all their quilts at the same time. Maybe make a celebration of it like we did for Summer Williams," Sarah suggested.

"Oh, I love that idea! Even though I'm not giving my project away, I'd like to be here for the others," Annalise said.

"Well, of course, you should be here. It wouldn't be right for you not to. You're just as much a part of the celebration as the rest of us. Besides, don't forget that you contributed to making Rachel's quilt," Jennifer reminded her.

"You're right. I did such a small piece of it that I didn't even think of my input. It still seems like it's your quilt, Jen."

"It's ours and that's what it's going to say on the label; pieced by Jennifer Ryder and Annalise Jordan."

Annalise reached out and squeezed Jennifer's hand.

"Have I told you recently how much I value your friendship? All of yours," Annalise said, turning to Eva and Sarah to include them.

"Awww. Group hug?" Eva asked and the four women stood with their arms encircling each other.

"Where's Reuben?" Sarah asked, looking around the room when they broke their embrace. "I can't believe I'm saying this, but I was missing his dissing us about our kumbaya moment."

"He's probably still sulking. He was pestering me for treats earlier today and I reminded him the vet said he needed to lose some weight. As you can imagine, that did not go over well," Eva said, chuckling.

"He has looked a bit rounder lately," Jennifer said, just as Reuben came into the room.

"Uh oh, busted," Sarah said when she spotted him.

He gave Jennifer a narrow-eyed glare and then turned and walked back to the living room.

"I think I offended him," Jennifer said, guiltily.

"Probably, but he'll get over it," Eva reassured her before switching gears. "Let's get quilting, ladies. We're on the home stretch."

CHAPTER 33

"We should go to Henry Ward's office today to see what he can tell us about Ted and Vinnie Barnes. He ought to be back from his vacation by now," Phil told Dennis.

"Great minds think alike," Dennis said and grabbed his jacket. "Let's go."

Henry Ward's accounting firm was located in downtown Bangor not far from the police station. It was a small office, but nicely decorated with a reception area, chairs for clients and coffee table with magazines and a copy of The Wall Street Journal. The only other employee was a receptionist who greeted them as soon as they walked in. The nameplate on her desk identified her as Chelsea Johnson. She was in her forties, dressed stylishly, and her hair and makeup were flawless.

"May I help you?" she asked smiling, but they could see in her eyes that she was confused about why they were there when she looked down at her appointment calendar and didn't see an entry for that time.

"Yes, we'd like to speak with Henry Ward. My name is Phil Roberts and my partner is Dennis Smith."

She gave them an assessing look before replying. "I'll check with Mr. Ward to see if he can see you now. I don't see an appointment scheduled for you, though, so he may not be able to squeeze you in."

"We understand." Dennis answered but his look let her know that they weren't about to leave until she checked with him.

Her frown reflected her displeasure, but she got up from her seat and walked to Henry's office. Knocking softly on the closed door, she opened it when they heard a mumbled 'yes?' She stepped into the office and shut the door. A moment later she reappeared with Henry behind her. He was a tall man, at least six feet four inches, in his early fifties, with dark hair that was beginning to show signs of gray. He had a puzzled expression as he approached and held out his hand first to Phil and then to Dennis.

"How can I help you gentlemen?" he asked.

This time they each took out their badges before introducing themselves. Henry's eyes widened and his demeanor changed from curiosity when he'd first approached them to nervousness.

"We'd like to ask you some questions about Vinnie Barnes and Ted Hartley. It shouldn't take too long," Phil told him.

"Chelsea, hold my calls," he addressed the receptionist before leading the detectives into his office and shut the door.

"I'm not sure what I can tell you. Ted was a friend of mine. He died in an accident while he was hunting back in November," Henry said, poker-faced, but a small bead of perspiration was forming on his hairline.

"We think there is more to it than that. We have information that you hired Ted Hartley to investigate Vinnie Barnes because he was blackmailing you," Dennis said.

Henry smiled but it didn't reach his eyes. "You must be mistaken. I had no reason to hire Ted, and Vinnie isn't blackmailing me. I'm his accountant. It's purely a professional relationship."

Phil and Dennis exchanged glances.

"Mr. Ward. We have evidence we received from Rachel

Hartley which her husband left for her. He had given it to his attorney with instructions to deliver it to her in case of his death."

"That's where it was," Henry said, shaking his head as he glanced down to avoid their eyes and his voice barely audible.

"I'm sorry. Are you saying you were looking for it?" Phil asked.

Henry met Phil's gaze and sighed.

"I might as well be honest with you. Yes, I was looking for it. It's not your department, but you may know there was a break in at Ted's office not long ago. I was the one who broke in. Vinnie found out that I'd hired Ted and threatened me and my family if I didn't get the file. I thought it might still be there. I wasn't going to do anything to Rachel. I swear."

"We believe you. We know you didn't try to enter their house," Dennis said.

"Why did you wait so long? It was two months after Ted's accident," Phil asked.

"I didn't know for sure that Vinnie was onto us. It was only a week after he started threatening me that I decided to look in Ted's office."

"What do you know about Ted's accident?" Dennis asked.

"At first I thought that's what it was although there was a part of me that knew it probably wasn't. At that point, I still believed we'd kept everything on the down low. Ted left me a voice mail the night before his accident. I saved it just in case. Would you like to hear it?"

"Definitely," Phil replied, leaning forward in his seat.

Henry opened a desk drawer and removed a cell phone. He navigated to the call and put the phone on Speaker so they all could hear.

"Be careful, Henry. I think he's onto us. He came to my office and threatened me."

Phil and Dennis glanced at each other, their eyebrows raised.

"And you didn't think that was connected to Ted's death?" Dennis asked.

"There was no way I could prove it even if it was. Ted didn't even mention Vinnie's name."

Phil nodded his head, acknowledging the logic.

"We have the proof now that the bolts were tampered with on the deer stand. Last week we went with the crime scene tech and he found them with a metal detector. They were tested at the lab and because of that we've been able to get the case opened as possible foul play. But we're going to need your testimony to take it to the next level. Would you be willing to come to the station to give us your statement?" Phil asked.

"I've got a wife to think about. If Vinnie is behind Ted's death, then she could be next if I go to the cops. He's already been threatening me. I thought I'd gotten free of him last year, but this has pulled me right back in. You've got to understand. I have to protect my family," Henry pleaded, looking to both of them for support.

"We can protect you. We have a lot of evidence, but it's circumstantial. We need your testimony to tie it back to Vinnie."

Henry sneered. "You have to know that he wouldn't have done this himself. He has people for that," he said, his voice scornful.

"Do you know who those people are?" Phil asked.

"I have some guesses, but that's all they are. It wouldn't hold up in court."

"Would you at least think about it? We believe we're very close to getting an arrest warrant. You've been working for him as his accountant. It's our understanding that murder isn't the only thing the DA's office is looking into. They know he's laundering money, too. Would you happen to know anything about that?"

Henry face blanched.

"I plead the Fifth."

Phil nodded. "We understand. What if we could get it in

writing from the DA's office that you wouldn't be held responsible if you agree to testify?"

"You could do that?" Henry asked.

"I can't guarantee it without speaking with them, but yeah, I'm pretty sure they'd be agreeable, especially knowing that you're being threatened and blackmailed," Dennis said.

"You get that in writing and I'll consider it."

"That's all we can ask for now. We'll be back in touch," Phil said, standing, and Dennis followed suit. "Thank you for your time, Mr. Ward."

"Watch your back. We'll try to get some extra protection for you and your family in the meantime," Dennis cautioned before following Phil out of the office.

The receptionist averted her eyes when she spotted them, a guilty expression on her face.

"Have a good day," Phil said, giving her a wave of his right hand.

"Um, you, too," she said, still concentrating on the file on her desk.

"Did she look a little off to you?" Dennis asked when they were outside the door.

"Yeah. Like she didn't want us to know what she was doing."

"Something to think about. Keep in the back of our minds," Dennis agreed.

"In the meantime, let's see if we can set up a meeting with Danielle Larson," Phil suggested.

"Great minds," Dennis replied.

CHAPTER 34

That was a long day. You're getting too old for this. Memo to self: don't schedule back-to-back appointments no matter how much a client says they need a session before your next opening. It's not good for you, and might not be the best for your client, either.

Annalise leaned her head back in her chair and let the music playing in the background calm her. She inhaled slowly through her nose and exhaled through her mouth to help the tension in her body release. Her thoughts melted away as she fell asleep, but her rest was soon interrupted as she began to lucid dream.

It's that vision again. No wait, something's different.

She saw two pairs of hands again but this time there was an envelope in one. He was handing it over and she heard a voice saying, "If anyone else talks..."

The dream ended and Annalise opened her eyes and sat upright, fully alert now. She grabbed her phone and hit the number for Phil Roberts.

"Phil, it's Annalise. Listen, Henry Ward might be in danger. I just had a vision and I'm positive it was Vinnie Barnes giving an envelope with money to another man. It was payment to make sure no one else talks."

"Has this already happened?" Phil asked.

Dennis looked up, tuning into the concern in Phil's voice.

"No, at least I don't think so. But it could happen soon."

CHAPTER 35

"Thanks for agreeing to see us, Danielle," Phil said.

"I hadn't planned to until you mentioned Vinnie Barnes. Your investigation may tie in with the one we're working on. Mike Nicholson is going to be joining us, too. You remember him from the Lily Sullivan matter, don't you?"

"Mike Nicholson? Sure. Why would he be involved in this?" Dennis asked.

"We're putting together a case against Vinnie for money laundering though his construction businesses. He took over the territory that Adam Parker had when he was arrested."

A knock sounded on the door and was immediately opened by Mike Nicholson before anyone had a chance to invite him in.

"Your assistant told me to just come in since you were expecting me," he addressed Danielle before noticing the detectives, whose backs had been to him. "Phil. Dennis. Great to see you again," he said, shaking their hands. "Aren't you still in homicide? I'm confused about why you're here."

"We were just going to get into that, but wanted to wait for you to arrive first. Let's sit over where it's more comfortable," Danielle suggested leading them to the couch and upholstered seating. She and Mike took the couch and Phil and Dennis sat in the chairs facing them.

Phil leaned forward, his elbows resting on his thighs. "Here's the Cliff notes version. Ted Hartley, a private investigator, was found dead after falling from a tree stand that collapsed. It was ruled an accident, but we recently had the bolts from the platform tested by the state crime lab. They'd been tampered with." He paused to let that sink in before continuing. "Ted was hired by Henry Ward, an accountant who's gotten tangled up with Vinnie Barnes. So far, we've pieced together that Barnes is blackmailing Henry so he'll keep working for him. He's doing that by creating a shell corporation to make it look like Henry's not just cooking the books, but laundering money through Vinnie's construction companies. Ted was getting close to providing that when he had his accident," Phil said, using air quotes.

"Do you remember Sarah Pascal from the Lily Sullivan case?" Dennis asked.

Mike nodded. "Of course."

"She's been helping us fill in some of the gaps of what Ted had collected. It's a long story, but Ted's widow, Rachel, is a mutual acquaintance of Sarah and Jessica Ryder, which is how she got involved."

"Do you have any solid proof Vinnie is behind Ted's murder?" Danielle asked.

"So far, it's mostly circumstantial, but Sarah is close. In fact, she was threatened anonymously and so was Rachel Hartley. They were both warned that they needed to stop looking into Ted's death."

Danielle's eyebrows raised questioningly and Dennis filled her in about the threats.

"We're here for two reasons. We'd like to make Sarah's findings official so they can be used when this goes to trial, and we're hoping you can help Henry Ward. Right now, he's afraid to testify because he and his family are being threatened. I think this could be urgent." He didn't elaborate on why he thought so, but hoped they believed him. "He's also worried the fake account would incriminate him. He'd like something in writing that no charges would be filed against him if he testifies. That's where you come in," Phil explained.

"Is that what you have so far?" Danielle asked, pointing to the envelope Dennis held.

"It is," Dennis replied handing it over to Danielle.

The men sat patiently while she looked through the paperwork.

"From what I'm seeing here, I wouldn't have a problem putting together an immunity agreement for Henry." She passed the file over to Mike.

"And authorizing Sarah to keep looking into this?" Phil asked.

"We'll need to have her coordinate with our team to ensure it will all be admissible, but yes, I think that can be done. Her work on the Sullivan case was outstanding and played an instrumental part in the Adam Parker arrest."

"We've talked to our boss about getting protection for Henry and his wife but he has to check to make sure there's money in the budget for anything more than extra drive-bys during regular shift times."

"I think this could really help solidify our investigation," Mike said, handing the envelope back to Dennis.

"I'll email you the agreement later today," Danielle said. "Do you think you could bring him here tomorrow?"

"As long as we have it in writing, I think we've got a good shot at it. Could your office help with the security piece? I'm thinking this might even need to get elevated to witness protection status, depending on what kind of influence you think Vinnie Barnes has. If he is the one behind Ted Hartley's death as a murder for hire, I don't think he'd hesitate to do it again if he thinks he can get away with it," Dennis said.

"We'll have to cross that bridge after we've had a chance to talk to Henry Ward and see how deep he's involved and how much of a threat he is to Barnes."

"Fair enough. Can we tell Sarah she's got the thumbs up to keep digging?"

"Yes, that's okay." Danielle took a piece of paper from her note pad and wrote down a name and phone number before handing it to Phil. "This is the contact info for Kevin Ross. Have her coordinate with him and I'll let him know to be expecting her call. Is this going to put her in more danger, though?"

"Knowing Sarah, it wouldn't stop her. Cyber security is her thing and I trust her to find a way to do this without getting caught."

"And what about Rachel Hartley?" Mike asked.

"She's not directly involved, but it's on us to make sure she doesn't get hurt."

"We're having patrols check on her, too. She's a teacher so should be safe while she's at work. Her neighbor is checking up on her when she's at home and she has a security system installed," Dennis said.

"The best way to protect her is to have Barnes behind bars." Phil said.

"Agreed. So let's get moving on that," Mike said.

CHAPTER 36

"Hey, Sarah, it's Phil Roberts. We met with Danielle Larson this morning and she's willing to bring you on board. We've got the name of a guy in her office she wants you to work with."

"Okay, I'm ready. What's his contact info?" Sarah asked, and Phil gave her Kevin Ross's information.

"We talked to Henry Ward yesterday and Danielle has agreed to give him immunity for his testimony. We're going to his office after we get off the phone with you to give him the copy of the agreement and take him to speak to her. Oh, almost forgot. Mike Nicholson is also on the case."

"No kidding? I guess that does make sense, though. If Barnes is laundering money, chances are drugs are involved," Sarah said. "It will be good to work with him again. He seems like a straight shooter. He was a big help with Lily's case."

"He sure was. We'll update you later after we've met with Henry Ward and Danielle."

"Thanks! Can't wait to hear what he has to say."

CHAPTER 37

hil and Dennis arrived at Henry Ward's office only to find it locked. A note was taped to the door saying it was closed due to family emergency, but no date for when it would reopen.

"I don't like the looks of this," Dennis said.

"Me either. I think we should go to his house," Phil said.

"I've got his address on my phone," Dennis said. "Here it is. It should only take us about ten minutes to get there."

They arrived at the cape style house in one of the nicer city neighborhoods a few minutes later. The door was answered by a fortyish woman who was clearly distraught.

"Mrs. Ward? I'm Detective Roberts and this is my partner, Detective Smith. Is your husband at home? We tried his office, but there was a sign saying there was a family emergency."

"What? I don't know where Henry is. I was just on my way to the police station to file a missing person's report. Come in, come in. You're letting all the heat out."

"A report? Why would you be doing that?" Dennis asked once they were inside.

"He hasn't come home. Last night Vinnie Barnes and another man I didn't recognize came to the house. They went into

Henry's office—the one he has here--for a few minutes so I didn't hear what they were saying. When they came out, they had Henry by the arms and he told me he had to take care of some business with them and he'd be back in a couple hours. But he never came home," she said, breaking down in tears.

"Do you have any idea where they might have gone?" Phil asked.

"Of course not. If I did, I'd have looked there already," she said, annoyance edging her voice.

"Have you tried calling him?"

She gave him a Captain Obvious look.

"Yes, and he isn't answering his phone. That's why I was on my way to the police station. Those men didn't look like it would be safe to go with them, but I could tell that Henry didn't have a choice just from the way they were holding his arms. And I saw the look in Henry's eyes. He was scared."

"We'll take care of the report for you," Dennis said. "If you hear from him, please let us know. Here's my card."

They were about to leave when Phil had a thought.

"You weren't the one to put the sign on his office door, were you?"

"No, of course not. It is a family emergency, but I'm not the one who put up the sign."

"Do you have any idea who did? Did you already talk to his receptionist about this?"

"Chelsea? No, I hardly know her. She's been working for Henry for about six months but I didn't have any reason to interact with her other than when I'd call the office. But I rarely did that because I could just text him if I needed to get in touch."

"Thank you, Mrs. Ward. We're going to look into this now."

"Please find him. I told Henry he should stop working for that Barnes guy but he said he couldn't. That's all he would say, though, and if I pressed him, he said it was better that he didn't tell me anything more for my safety."

"We'll find him, ma'am." Phil reassured her before they stepped outside.

"Are you sure you should have told her that?" Dennis asked quietly, even though the door was already closed behind them.

"I didn't say we'd find him alive. But I sure hope we do," Phil said, grimly.

CHAPTER 38

"Phil and Dennis called me this afternoon to tell me that Henry Ward is missing," Sarah announced at the weekly meeting.

"I warned them this might happen," Annalise said.

"What?" three shocked voices answered.

"I had a dream that Vinnie was paying someone to make sure no one else would talk. I called Phil to tell him I thought it might be Henry who was in danger. They must not have gotten to him quickly enough."

"They had an immunity agreement from Danielle Larson to testify against Vinnie, but his office was closed and his wife told them he'd been taken away last night by Vinnie and one of his *associates*," Sarah said, using air quotes.

"Oh, my goodness. What about you? Does this have you more worried after getting that text?" Eva asked.

"I'd be lying if I said no, but I've been a lot more careful not to leave any fingerprints behind. The guys said they're going to have patrols go by my house more regularly. That made me feel better about coming tonight. I didn't want to leave Ashley alone, but she insisted I should come. She has their number on speed dial and she can always call 911. I told her to call them first, though, because they'd get someone to our house faster."

"That was smart thinking. I'm really starting to regret telling you about this. Here it was me that David was worried about, but you've been putting yourself out on the line much more than I have, Sarah," Jennifer said, a concerned look on her face.

"We've all put ourselves out before and it's been okay. My intuition is telling me it will be fine this time, too," Sarah replied.

"I'm with Sarah on this," Annalise said. "I'm not getting any vibes otherwise. That's not saying there might not be some excitement, but I don't get the sense that it will be dangerous for us personally before this is over."

"What about Rachel? Is she okay, too?" Eva asked, her forehead furrowed.

Annalise thought for a moment, searching her intuition and then shaking her head. "I don't feel any danger there either. My gut is saying that this will all be over soon and Vinnie won't be able to harm anyone--even indirectly." She added, before someone could mention that he wasn't directly responsible for Ted's death.

Eva blew out her breath at that news.

"Your gut is good enough for me," she said.

"Me, too," Sarah and Jennifer said in unison.

"Is there anything we can be doing to help, Sarah?" Jennifer asked.

"I don't think so, Jen. Phil and Dennis are going to be taking over most of the case now. The only thing I still need is the identity of the person who got the money from the shell corporation. Danielle put me in touch with a guy on her staff, so between the two of us, I don't think it will take long. Now that that's settled, how about we get dinner? I'm starving. I forgot to eat lunch today and the smell of that beef stew is making my stomach growl."

"Good idea," Eva replied.

Did someone say food? Reuben trotted into the dining room

where the ladies were gathered, but was disappointed when he saw the empty table. *Call me when it's ready,* he said to Eva before walking back to the living room.

"Not going to happen," she called out after him.

Meow

"That one's not suitable for translation," she said, her eyes round, eliciting a chuckle from the others. "Now he's *definitely* not getting any treats."

"Did you make the bread, Annalise?" Sarah asked. She picked up a warm slice and held it up to her nose to inhale its scent. "It's a sourdough, isn't it?"

"I did. And, yes, it's a sourdough that I thought would go well with the stew. If anyone needs a starter, I can bring some next week. I've got plenty to spare."

"If you bring along the recipe for the bread, too, I'd love to have some," Sarah said. "Oh, and instructions for how to keep it going, although Ashley probably knows what to do."

"I'd like to try it, too," Eva said. "Someday I'm going to find the instructions for the starter for friendship bread. You two are probably too young to remember, but Annalise might. It was a thing in the seventies, just like sourdough became during COVID. At least we didn't have a worldwide pandemic to go along with it, though."

"I hadn't thought of that in years, but I do remember now that you mention it," Annalise said. "I bet you can find the recipe on the internet. There isn't much you can't find with a quick browser search."

"Well, duh. Why had that not occurred to me?" Eva asked. "I'm going to do that tomorrow. Assuming I don't forget between now and then," she said, rolling her eyes.

"I think my mom had that starter when I was a teenager back in the nineties. It must have had a comeback," Jennifer said.

"Okay, you have me curious. What's friendship bread?" Sarah asked.

"It's made from a sourdough starter, but you feed it differently and it's a sweeter dough. You can make all sorts of things besides bread despite its name, if I'm remembering correctly," Eva said.

"You are. I made a cinnamon coffee cake once, or maybe several times with my starter," Annalise said, smiling, "I finally tossed it because my life was busy at the time and I didn't want to keep feeding it. Tell you what, Eva, I'll trade you starters once you get yours ready."

"It's a deal."

"I think I'd like to try that, too, if you have enough to share," Jennifer said.

"It sounds delicious. I should ask Ashley first if we have a spot to store two starters. I'd feel guilty if I took it and wasn't able to keep it alive," Sarah said.

"In the meantime, you're welcome to eat the goodies I make from mine," Eva said, patting Sarah's arm.

"Works for me, and probably Ashley, too," she replied, grinning widely.

"When it's time for the quilting session, I want to show you Vivian's," Sarah said. I ended up taking it to Nicki for the quilting part and I lucked out. She had a free stretch of time so it only took a few days to get it back. I'm going to do the trimming and binding tonight and then it will be ready to give to Vivian. Are we still on to do a celebration of life ceremony with Rachel, Vivian, and Meghan?"

"Absolutely, Sarah. I was thinking we can invite our significant others, too, and make a party of it," Eva suggested. "Do you think you could have yours ready in a couple weeks, Jennifer? We should set a date since Vivian has to travel from Massachusetts, but if you need more time, that's fine."

Jennifer thought for a moment.

"I think I could and with a deadline, I'd make sure I got it finished. I've already got my appointment scheduled with Evelyn to use the longarm machine. Once that's done, it wouldn't take more than a day or two to do the binding. I'd rather hand sew it to finish it. I never seem to manage to get the stitching straight when I try to do that on the machine and my perfectionism kicks in. It's one thing when it's for me, but this is a keepsake so I want it to look right."

"Why don't I call Vivian and Meghan to ask what their schedules are like and have her tell me when it would work for them. But no sooner than two weeks away," Sarah added in a rush when she saw the look of panic in Jennifer's eyes.

"I think that's a wonderful idea. Let's come back to this next week after we've all had a chance to think about planning the party," Eva said.

"Sounds like a plan," Jennifer said and was seconded by Annalise and Sarah.

CHAPTER 39

"I think we need to track down that receptionist," Phil said. "Did you get her name?"

"It's Chelsea something. I wrote it down." Dennis pulled out the small spiral notebook from his suit jacket pocket and flipped to the page. "It's Chelsea Johnson. We'll need to get an address."

"Let's try DMV records to see if she's got a license." Phil put the info into his computer and was rewarded with the correct one when the picture matched that of Chelsea Johnson. He scribbled down the information on a piece of note paper and grabbed his jacket that was hanging on the back of his chair. "Got it. She lives here in Bangor. Let's go see if she's home. I'm guessing she's the one who left the sign on the office door and chances are she hasn't already got another job. Or skipped town."

"Fingers crossed," Dennis agreed.

"We might have gotten lucky. There's a car in the driveway," Phil said, when they pulled up to the ranch style house. All of the curtains were drawn shut, giving the house an abandoned appearance.

"It was my crossed fingers," Dennis joked and received a side eye response.

"You might need to cross your fingers again," Phil told him when there was no answer to their knocks on the door.

Just as they were turning to leave, Dennis reached out his arm to stop Phil. He nodded his head in the direction of one of the windows at the far end of the house. "I saw a hand pulling back the curtain at that window so they could take a look at us. I think whoever was there saw me because they pulled it back in."

"We're going to play that game, huh?" Phil said, looking toward the window Dennis pointed out. This time he knocked even harder and rather than waiting for someone to answer the door, called out. "We know you're here Ms. Johnson. It's Detectives Roberts and Smith. We met at Henry Ward's office and we know you're involved in whatever is going on. We can do this here or we can come back with a warrant to take you downtown. My partner will wait here to make sure you don't decide to leave."

Dennis gave him a *what the heck* look but Phil just shook his head to reassure him he didn't think it would come to that. They barely recognized her when less than a minute later, the door was opened by a disheveled looking Chelsea Johnson. There were circles under her red-rimmed eyes, her hair needed brushing, and she wore no makeup.

"What do you want?" she asked with some defensiveness in her tone.

"May we come in?" Phil asked, but in a way that showed her saying no wasn't an option.

She stepped aside to let them in and then looked up and down the street before closing the door as though she was checking to see if anyone was watching. She directed them to the living room to the left of the door. Dirty dishes and a box of tissues accompanied by piles of used ones littered the coffee table.

"I haven't been feeling well," Chelsea said, still on the defensive.

"We need to speak with you about Henry Ward's disappearance," Dennis began.

"What do you mean his disappearance? The office is closed for a family emergency. His wife called to let me know and asked me to put the note on the door," she said.

Had they not known better, her response might have been believable.

"We know that's not true. We've already spoken to his wife. She doesn't know where he is either and he's been missing since the day we came to his office. How are you connected to Vinnie Barnes?"

The question caught her off-guard and she recoiled as her eyes widened with fear. She opened her mouth to speak and then closed it. Tried one more time with the same results.

"Has Vinnie Barnes threatened you somehow?" Phil asked on a hunch.

She nodded her head several times and clasped her hands in her lap. Taking a deep breath, she began to speak. "I have a gambling addiction and owed some money that I couldn't repay. He had one of his guys threaten me that if I didn't cooperate, I'd be sorry. All I had to do so he'd rip up my IOU was to work for Henry and report back to them on who came and went. I think they told him to hire me to make sure I got the job. They gave me a bug that I hid under his desk so they could listen in. After you came to talk to him, they came here and told me Henry would be gone for a while and I should put up the sign saying the office would be closed."

"Who's they?" Phil asked.

"I don't know his name, but I know he works for Vinnie. He's the same one who came to threaten me in the first place."

"How would you describe him?"

"He's about six feet tall, stocky build, with dark brown hair and eyes. He's got acne scars."

"Do you think you could work with a sketch artist so we would have a composite to use to identify him?" Dennis asked.

"Only if I absolutely have to. They could be watching my house right now. I could end up like Henry." Realizing she'd said too much, she clamped her lips in a thin line.

"Do you know what's happened to him or where he is? Earlier, you said they just told you he'd be gone for a few days," Phil said, his voice harsh.

"I don't know for sure," she hedged. "They probably took him to one of the job sites to scare him so he wouldn't testify like you want him to."

"Which job site?" Dennis demanded.

"I don't know. They've got a bunch."

"Ms. Johnson, it's beginning to sound like you know more than you're admitting," Phil said. "We can still take you to the station. Even if they're not watching the house, they could have someone on the inside who could leak it to Barnes that you're cooperating with us."

"You're no better than they are," she snarled. "Either way I'm the one who's going to get screwed."

The tension in the room was palpable.

"We can make you the same deal that we did for Henry. I'm sure the DA's office will put it in writing for you," Dennis said.

"Do you have like a safe house or something where I can stay until everyone is arrested?" she asked, less belligerently.

The men exchanged glances and Phil subtly lifted his shoulders.

"I think we can arrange that," Dennis replied. "In the meantime, we can have extra patrol cars check on you."

"That didn't do Henry much good, did it?"

Her point wasn't lost on them.

"Let me make a phone call to the DA's office now and set something up so you can go with us and you won't be left here alone."

She met his gaze, leveling her eyes on his. At last, convinced he meant what he was saying, she nodded. "Okay."

"I'll go out to the car to make the call. Detective Smith will wait here with you."

Fifteen minutes later Phil returned. Dennis raised his eyebrows, silently asking if he'd been successful and got a nod in the affirmative.

"It's all arranged. For now, a female police officer is being assigned to stay with you inside your residence and an unmarked vehicle will be placed outside to watch your house. We'll transfer you to a safe house by tomorrow afternoon. The DA's office will write up an immunity agreement for you to sign. Which, by the way, they did for Henry Ward. That's why we were at the office and his house—we planned to give it to him, but he was already gone. We learned our lesson which is why the DA put this together so quickly."

He turned to Dennis.

"We'll stay here with Ms. Johnson until Officer Dietz gets here. She's on her way so it shouldn't take long."

A woman in civilian clothes knocked at the door ten minutes later and Phil went to answer. After introductions were made, he and Dennis left to take the next step.

"Sorry it took me so long. I didn't want to say anything in front of her, but I got in touch with Sarah to make a list of the construction sites Vinnie Barnes is working at now. There are about eleven, which is more than I was hoping for, but I think we can narrow it down. We'll get teams on board to do searches and you better cross those lucky fingers again that we find him before it's too late."

Dennis held up both hands with his fingers crossed.

CHAPTER 40

"Are you sure we're on the right track? We've already been to five of the sites on the list and we haven't found him," Dennis asked, his voice reflecting his discouraged attitude.

They were standing in front of an empty construction site that looked like it hadn't been operating for some time. He was there with Phil and Mike Nicholson and a backup team of officers. A trailer for use by the site manager was situated in the far corner of the gated lot.

"Let's find out," Mike replied, pulling out his bolt cutters and clamping them around the lock securing the metal gate. There was a rattle of metal on metal as the lock broke and the length of heavy links holding it in place unraveled, clattering to the ground.

They approached the trailer, but the door was padlocked. Mike cut through the lock and handed the cutters over to Phil. He turned the handle, but it was locked, too. "They weren't taking any chances," he muttered under his breath. From inside his jacket, he took a set of tools to unlock the door.

"You've had some practice with that," Phil said, his eyebrows raised upon seeing the speed at which it took him to open the door.

"A little," Mike answered, grinning.

Phil and Mike were the closest to the entry and reflexively covered their noses and mouths when the stench of body odor and human waste greeted them as soon as they opened the door. Their eyes met in a look of concern.

"You first," Mike said.

CHAPTER 41

"What'll you have?" Betty Jones asked, with her pencil poised over her order pad.

"I'll have the Cobb salad with a vinegarette dressing on the side, please," Eva said.

"Cheeseburger and fries for me," Jim told her.

"I'd like the Reuben and fries," Liam said.

"So would Reuben," Eva quipped. "That's my cat's name," she explained to Betty. "He thinks I'm starving him because I've cut back his food treats. He was getting a little chubby."

"I've got one like that, too," she said. "It's for their own good. What about you, Annalise?"

Annalise was about to tell her she didn't have a cat, but changed her mind. Betty's matter-of-fact personality didn't always respond to joking.

"The haddock looks good. I'll have a side salad with ranch dressing to go with it, please."

"Coming right up." Betty tucked the pencil behind her ear and marched toward the kitchen to give the order to Sam, the diner's short-order cook.

"Look at us taking time off in the middle of the day," Annalise said, gently poking Liam's arm.

"My boss was in a good mood today," Liam replied with a big grin.

Eva and Jim were in on the joke, knowing that both Annalise and Liam were self-employed.

"Have you heard from the detectives about Henry Ward?" Jim asked Eva, keeping his voice low to avoid being overheard.

"This is the case I told you about," Annalise enlightened Liam when she saw his confused expression.

"Gotcha," he nodded, getting the connection.

"Not a peep since Sarah told us he was missing," Eva said.

Annalise felt a tingling in her arms and closed her eyes. In her mind's eye, she saw the trailer with the detectives and Mike Nicholson standing at the door, and then the vision disappeared. She opened her eyes to find herself the center of attention as all eyes were on her.

"I think they just found him… or are about to. They're at a construction site."

Eva leaned forward toward Annalise and whispered, "Is he okay?"

"I didn't see that part of what's happening. My intuition is telling me he's there, though."

CHAPTER 42

Phil pressed his lips together and narrowed his eyes at Mike, expressing his displeasure but stepped into the trailer. The lighting inside was dim, but he was able to make out the expected setup of a mobile office. A small table was scattered with blueprints and papers related to the building construction and banquette seating behind the table stretched across the width of the trailer. A kitchenette with microwave, stove, sink, and refrigerator was adjacent to the seating area. Phil looked to his left down a hallway that led to a bedroom and sprawled across the bed with his wrists handcuffed to metal rings attached to the wall he saw the figure of a man. His stomach tightened when there was no response from the man to having someone enter the trailer.

"Oh, no," Phill muttered under his breath before sprinting to the back of the trailer. He placed his fingers on the man's throat and felt a pulse, weak but there. His face was bruised and battered and his eyes were swollen shut. He moaned in pain when he felt Phil's touch.

"No more, please," Henry mumbled through his swollen lips.

"Henry, it's Detective Roberts. Hang on, buddy, we're going to get you out of here." Turning, he shouted to the men still standing at the doorway. "Call for an ambulance. He's alive but he's banged up pretty bad."

Dennis pulled out his phone and made the call.

"Water, please," Henry croaked, his voice barely above a whisper.

"Is there any water in that refrigerator?" Phil called out.

Mike found a bottle in the fridge and took it to Phil.

"Is it Ward?" he asked quietly.

"Yeah," Phil replied. "We need to get these cuffs off him first." He used his key to unlock them and Henry groaned again as his wrists were released from the cuffs. Phil gently moved Henry's arms down to his sides and gingerly sat on the bed to prop him up to drink. "Just sips," he cautioned when he tried to gulp the water.

"Thanks," Henry said, his voice clearer, but still raspy.

Phil and Mike looked up as they heard the sound of an ambulance siren approaching.

"I'll ride with him to the hospital. You and Dennis meet me there," Phil said, and Mike nodded his assent before walking back to update Dennis.

"Come on, we should get outside to make way for the EMTs. Phil told us to meet him at the hospital. He's going to ride with Ward. We need to get there ahead of him to make sure we've got security set up for Ward."

"You okay for me to leave? The ambulance just pulled into the lot," Dennis called out to Phil, who was still sitting on the bed supporting Henry.

"Yeah. Let the backup team know they can leave, too. No, on second thought, someone should be watching the site to see who comes back to check on it," Phil replied. "The ambulance is here. You're going to be okay," he told Henry, who only nodded his head slowly. "Who did this to you, Henry?"

There was no response, and Phil briefly panicked until he realized Henry was still alive, but unconscious.

He gently laid Henry down on the bed and walked to the

front of the trailer to wait for the EMTs and directed them to the bedroom as soon as they arrived. Sitting on the banquette, he put his face in his hands as his elbows rested on his thighs, and let out a deep sigh.

This guy could have been killed. We didn't do enough to protect him.

He didn't have long to wallow in his guilt before the medical team returned with Henry on a gurney.

"I'm riding with him," Phil told them.

"Understood."

They arrived at the hospital Emergency entrance within five minutes and wheeled Henry straight into a room where an ER doctor was waiting. Phil knew the drill and stood discreetly in a spot out of their way while they administered to Henry's injuries.

"He's going to be okay, but we're going to admit him for the night to make sure he's stabilized. We're going to take some X-rays to make sure there's nothing broken, but he's pretty dehydrated and it's going to take a while for the swelling to go down," the doctor said, looking in Phil's direction and then walked over and lowered his voice. "Is he a prisoner?"

"No, a witness. We're going to put an officer outside his room."

"Got it. We'll need his full name and emergency contact info."

"His name is Henry Ward and his wife's name is Celia. I've got their home phone number if you don't already have it in your records. Can we talk to him now?" he asked, once the doctor had written down the details.

"No, I've given him a heavy-duty pain killer that's going to put him out for a while. You can check back in a few hours and we'll see how he's doing. We'll call his wife."

Phil nodded and left to find Dennis and Mike, knowing there was nothing more for him to do. He found them in the ER waiting area.

"How's he doing?" Dennis asked.

"The doc says he'll be okay. They're keeping him overnight for observation and get him hydrated. It will be longer if the X-rays show any broken bones. They're going to notify Henry's wife. I let him know we're placing a guard outside the room but that Henry's not a prisoner, he's a witness."

"I've got that set up. How long before they get him into a room?"

"You know how that is. Could be minutes. Could be hours. We should check on his wife, though. If Vinnie knows we've got Henry, he could go after her for leverage to make sure he doesn't talk."

"You guys go. I'll wait here until the protection duty arrives."

"Thanks, Mike, for everything. Can you let Danielle know what's happened?"

"Sure. I'll do that right now," he said, pulling out his phone.

Dennis patted him on his shoulder. "Thanks."

CHAPTER 43

Phil and Dennis walked out of the ER, both with their shoulders slumped as the weight of the day fell on them.

"You drive," Dennis said, tossing the keys to Phil, who nearly missed catching them because he wasn't fully paying attention.

"I don't th..." he started to object, but realized that was exactly why Dennis gave him the assignment. *Right. It will take my mind off this to get me focused on what to do next,* he thought.

Celia Ward answered the door with her keys in her hand before they'd even knocked. She jumped, startled to see them standing there.

"I can't talk now. I've got to get to the hospital. Henry's been hurt," she said, brushing past them.

"We know. We're the ones who found him. But you could be in danger, too. Vinnie Barnes hasn't been arrested yet and we don't want him using you to intimidate Henry," Dennis explained.

Her surprised expression turned to fear.

"What do you mean?"

"You know Vinnie took your husband along with the man

who was with him. They beat him up pretty bad and had him at one of Vinnie's construction sites. When they find out Henry's not there, they might come after you. We'll take you to the hospital to make sure you get there safely."

Celia nodded, her lips pressed together and her eyes watered with the tears waiting to spill out. She put her keys back in her purse and allowed the men to lead her to their car. Dennis sat in the back seat with her while Phil drove. Neither man spoke, respecting Celia's time to process their news, but Dennis texted to let Mike know they were on their way.

Mike greeted them in the waiting room of the ER and Phil introduced him to Celia.

"They just took Henry up to a room." He started to tell them the room number but stopped, not wanting to be overheard as a precautionary safety measure. "Follow me."

When the four of them were in the elevator, Dennis asked, "Is the guard there?"

"Yeah, I sent him up with Henry so there wasn't any time he was alone."

"Thank you," Celia told him, gratefully.

"Of course, ma'am. We're not going to let Vinnie Barnes get away with this," Mike said, leveling his eyes on hers. "We're already working on making sure of that."

She continued to look him in the eyes for a moment before nodding. "I believe you."

The elevator doors slid open and they followed the room number locator signs to Henry's room where the guard was sitting in a folding chair outside the door. He came to attention when he spotted the group walking in his direction and his hand drifted toward his duty belt but returned to his side as he stood when he recognized the officers.

"We're going to leave now, but Officer O'Toole will be here. I'm sure you'd like some time alone with Henry," Phil said.

"Yes, thank you," Celia said, and took a deep breath before

opening the door. She stopped suddenly as she crossed the threshold, gasped, and her hand flew to her mouth, when she saw Henry lying in the bed with IV tubes attached to his arm and the bruises on his face.

CHAPTER 44

"'m going to text Annalise and Jennifer to let them know we've got Henry," Phil said as they walked through the lobby and out the main entrance of the hospital.

"Good idea. In all the excitement, I forgot they might be worried knowing that he was missing," Dennis said.

"Done," Phil said and almost immediately heard two pings in reply. "They said thank you and are relieved to hear it," he reported to Dennis.

———

"Oh, thank goodness!" Jennifer told Eva when she got the text. They were in Eva's sewing studio, working on their quilts.

"Should we tell Rachel? Her car's in the driveway so she must be home."

"Yes, I think she'd want to know about this," Jennifer agreed and dialed her number. "Rachel, are you busy? I'm here at Eva's house and we'd like to come see you. We have some good news."

They were greeted at Rachel's door a few minutes later by Rachel and a very excited Finn.

"Come on, boy, let them in," Rachel said, tugging gently on his collar to give them room to enter when he didn't move.

"Hello, Finn. How are you?" Eva said, leaning down to stroke his head.

"He's been anxious lately and barking more at night," Rachel replied for him. "He's probably picking up on my anxiety. I know the sheriff's office has been patrolling more often because I've seen their cars, but until this is resolved…"

"We understand. That's one of the reasons we're here. We just heard from Phil Roberts that they've found Henry Ward. He's in the hospital but he's going to be okay."

"Does this mean it's almost over?"

"He didn't say, but it must be getting close. Now that there's an immunity agreement, Henry is sure to testify."

Finn ran to the couch and jumped up to look out the window facing the street. His head swiveled quickly to the right and then left as he surveyed the street and he began to bark.

"See what I mean?" Rachel asked and walked toward the couch.

"Why don't I ask him what has him so worried?" Eva offered.

Rachel stopped in her tracks. "Oh, right. I forgot you can talk to animals."

Eva went to Finn's side and looked out the window. He was now growling low in his throat with his head turned to the left.

"There's a car parked across the street. Do you know anyone who drives a blue Ford Bronco?"

"I assume you're asking me," Rachel said, keeping her tone light. "But the answer is I don't know anyone who owns one of those. Let me take a closer look."

She walked to the other side of Finn and peeked out the window. A man looked over at them from the driver's side and when he realized he was being watched, he gunned the engine and sped off.

"Did you get a good look at him?" Eva asked her.

"He had brown hair, I think, but it could have been black. I know it was dark, though. He didn't look young. I mean, not like someone in their twenties."

"That's what I saw, too. I think we should call Deputy Tremblay and report it," Jennifer suggested. "It could be nothing but with all that's going on, we shouldn't leave it to chance."

"Agreed." Eva said.

"Finn, have you seen that car before?"

Yes, it stopped yesterday and the day before. I think they were looking at Ted's office more than they were looking at the house.

Eva translated for Rachel and Jennifer.

Rachel's face paled.

"Do you think they're going to try to break in again?"

"I hope not. I still think we should call Deputy Tremblay and see what he thinks," Jennifer said and called 911.

"Why don't you come stay with me for a few days until we get this sorted out?" Eva suggested.

"I don't want to impose. And does Reuben get along with dogs? I wouldn't feel right leaving Finn here by himself."

"You know, that's a good question. I don't know if he's ever been around dogs. But he'll just have to figure it out because your safety is more important than whether he can get along with Finn," Eva said. "Speaking of Finn, how are you with cats?"

I like them! Finn said, with a doggie smile.

Eva was about to translate but stopped when Jennifer began to speak.

"Deputy Tremblay, I'm so glad I got through to you. I'm at Rachel Hartley's house and a Blue Bronco just parked across the street from her driveway. When the driver realized we'd seen him, he drove off in a hurry." She paused to listen. "Yes, we'll wait until you can get here." She disconnected the call. "He'll be here in about ten minutes. He was already on this side of town."

Rachel's shoulders relaxed at the news. "We may as well get comfortable in the meantime. Can I get either of you something to drink?"

"Not for me, but would you like to put together some things while we're waiting?" Eva asked.

Rachel was quiet for a moment as she reconsidered the invitation.

"I appreciate your offer, Eva, but I think I'll be fine. I'm making sure to set the security alarm every night and I have Finn, too. And Ted taught me some things about protecting myself."

"Alright, but if you change your mind…" Eva let the invitation hang in the air.

"I will," Rachel said, meeting Eva's eyes and letting her know she meant it.

Finn barked even before the women realized the deputy had arrived.

"See what I mean? He's just as good as my security system," Rachel joked and went to open the door. Finn remained sitting beside Eva, confident that Rachel was meeting a friend not a foe.

"Good afternoon, ladies," Tremblay said upon seeing Jennifer and Eva. "Jennifer told me you've had someone suspicious here?" he addressed Rachel.

She gave him the description of the car and the man driving while he wrote it down in his spiral notebook.

"You didn't happen to get the license plate number?" he asked.

Both Eva and Rachel shook their heads.

"When he was parked, we could only see the side of the vehicle and he drove away so quickly, I wasn't able to make out all of the numbers, but it started with one five and the last letter was a P," Eva told him.

"I'll put in the report and make sure the officer on duty tonight makes some additional rounds past your house and if he has a little extra time, would you be okay with him parking in your driveway? If this guy comes back and sees the patrol car, it might be enough to keep him from coming back again."

"Thank you so much and, of course, it's more than okay for him to park in my driveway."

"Well, that's all I can do for now. You ladies, stay alert and stay safe."

Jennifer checked her watch. "I should probably go now, too. Are you sure you'll be okay?"

"Ninety-nine percent," Rachel said with a smile.

"I'll walk back with you, Jen. Your purse is still inside my house." She gave Rachel a last appraising glance before saying goodbye. "Take good care of her, Finn."

Woof!

Eva spied Reuben stretched out on the couch when she and Jennifer returned for her purse.

"You dodged a bullet today, Reuben. You almost had to share the house with Finn, but it all worked out."

Reuben's eyes widened and he sprang up onto all fours. *You were going to bring a dog here?*

"I offered a friend a safe place to stay," Eva replied.

Reuben stared at her and for once he was speechless.

CHAPTER 45

The detectives didn't hear from the hospital until the next morning that it was okay for them to speak with Henry. When they arrived, he was sitting up in his bed and some of the swelling had gone down in his face. Celia was sitting in a chair pulled up close to the bed, holding his hand.

"You're looking a lot better than you did yesterday," Phil said.

"Thank you for rescuing me. I honestly thought I was going to die there," his speech came out slurred but his lips curved up into as much of a smile as he could manage.

"You're welcome. Do you think you could tell us what happened? Your wife has already told us that Vinnie and another man are the ones who took you from your house, so you can start from what happened after that," Dennis said.

"They'd heard our conversation in my office. My receptionist was working for Vinnie and put a listening device under my desk."

"She confessed that to us. We have her in protection now and she's agreed to testify against him. He had blackmailed her to do it, but the DA will give her the same deal as she's giving you. We brought the paperwork you requested with us. We'll get to that later, though."

"Who's the guy who was with Vinnie?" Dennis interrupted. He had his notebook at the ready.

"His name is Arthur O'Donnell. He works on Vinnie's construction crew, but he's also one of his enforcers. I'm pretty sure he's got a record. He might be the one who rigged the platform that Ted fell from."

Dennis wrote down the name and added a note to give it to Sarah to see if he was the one attached to the murder for hire payout.

"Vinnie told me he'd put an alert on the bank account he'd set up to blackmail me and when Ted accessed it, he hired his own PI. He had pictures of Ted and me exchanging documents and they'd hacked Ted's email so they knew it was me who hired him. I told you about the voice mail saying he'd finally got the proof we needed. He never had the chance to give it to me but after he died, I figured that would be the end of it. It was lucky I didn't take that phone with me or they would have destroyed it."

"But I tried calling you. I didn't hear your phone ring," Celia said, her confusion evident.

"I had my personal phone with me. Ted and I used burner phones to communicate with each other," he explained.

"Was the proof on his laptop?" Phil asked.

"I couldn't get into it. He'd encrypted the password and I'm no IT guy. I thought about destroying the hard drive but something made me hold off. It's in the wall safe at my house along with the burner phone. It's okay to give the laptop and phone to them if I don't get out of here today, Celia."

"But I don't want to leave you…"

"It's okay, honey. I've got the guard right outside my door."

"We could take you, Mrs. Ward, and bring you right back. It's probably best you don't do that when you're alone," Phil offered.

Celia looked at Henry who nodded his approval. "That's a good idea Celia. I don't want that thing in the house anymore."

"While we have both of you here, this is the immunity agreement the DA's office prepared. Why don't you look it over and we'll try to answer any questions you might have," Dennis said.

"You'll have to read it to me. My eyes are still too swollen and the words are blurry," Henry said, handing the document to Celia.

She began reading it aloud, but when she got to the part about witness protection services, a panicked look came over her face and she looked up at Henry.

"You can't be serious. You're actually thinking about us having to change our identities and move away from everything and everyone we know? Henry, I don't think I could do that. Please don't say we have to," she pleaded.

"There's another option, Mrs. Ward. We could place you in a safe house until the trial and after Barnes is sent to prison, you could return to your home and your life," Phil assured her. "That's in the next part of the agreement."

"Oh," she replied, flustered. "I didn't read that far. How long would that be?"

"We wish we could tell you but it all depends on how quickly we get a court date and that's a question the DA's office would be better able to answer. To be perfectly honest with you, though, it could be a few months or as long as a year."

"How would we live in the meantime? I wouldn't be able to work," Henry asked. "I could lose all my clients," he said realizing the extent of the consequences.

"I'm sorry to be blunt, but this is for your safety. It would still be better than being dead," Dennis said.

"Way to be diplomatic," Phil muttered under his breath.

Henry sighed and took Celia's hand.

"I'll do whatever you want, babe."

"Don't put this all on me. We need to decide this together," Celia answered.

"You're right. It will be both our decisions. But what do you think?"

The only sound in the room was the beeping of the monitors as she considered the options.

"I don't like it, but I agree with the detective. It would be better than being killed by Vinnie. Of the two options, I'd rather try the safe house first. I can't imagine giving up our lives to become someone new and starting all over again."

Henry thought it over. "Yeah, that's what I think, too. If we do the safe house but find out it's been compromised, can we choose the witness protection?"

"I may have misspoken before. Sorry, if I confused you. The witness protection wouldn't come into play until after the trial. You'd have to be available to testify, but that's where the safe house would come in," Phil clarified. "Is there any way you could conduct your business remotely? Do you have to physically be with your clients?"

"Maybe it could work that way," Henry considered. "Do we have to be at a safe house if we go out-of-state? We have a condo in Florida we could move to temporarily."

"We know someone who specializes in cyber security. We can ask if there's a way to set something up so your location would be protected."

"What do you think, Celia? Would you like to go to Florida for a while?"

"As long as I'm with you, I'm good."

"Okay. Hand me a pen so I can sign this."

CHAPTER 46

Even before the knock on her door, Max was off like a shot and Sarah had been too surprised to catch him. She ran down the stairs after him and saw two men standing at her front door, but she recognized them instantly.

"Settle down, Max. It's Phil and Dennis. Sit."

He gave her a doleful look but sat while she opened the door.

"Stay," she warned, pointing her finger at him, when she noticed his hind end inching off the floor.

"We've got a present for you," Phil announced and handed her the laptop, then went to give Max attention.

"Is this what I think it is?"

"Depends. What do you think it is?" Dennis teased.

"You two are in a good mood today. I'm guessing this is Ted Hartley's laptop, but how did you get it?"

They gave her the salient points of their meeting with Henry and Celia Ward and the name of the man who'd helped Vinnie to kidnap Henry.

"Do you think you can unlock the password?" Dennis asked.

She scowled at him.

"Just asking," Dennis said, holding up his palms, but was smiling.

"Do you have time to wait while I try?" she asked.

Phil looked at his watch.

"Would half an hour be enough?"

"Let's go find out. Come on Max," she said leading the way to her office.

After ten minutes of trying, Sarah sat back in her chair to think. The detectives had been playing with Max, but gave her their full attention.

"This is taking me longer than I thought it would. Ted was more tech savvy than I was giving him credit for. I'm not giving up, though. There's another more advanced program I can try."

"While we're waiting, we have another situation we're hoping you can help with," Dennis said.

"You've got my curiosity piqued. What do you need?" Sarah asked.

"Is there a way to shield Henry Ward's location if he and his wife hide out at their condo in Florida until the trial?"

"I assume you mean without having them be in witness protection or I wouldn't be the one you're asking."

"You assume correctly," Phil replied.

They waited patiently while Sarah considered the possibilities.

"Yeah, I think we can do that. Is Danielle on board with this?"

"Not at first, but we told her it was the only way Henry would sign the agreement to testify," Dennis said.

"I'll work with Kevin Ross on it once I get the official word from Danielle's office."

"Thanks, Sarah. If anyone can do it, it's you," Phil said.

"Thanks. Do you have anything else about Arthur O'Donnell you can share?"

"He goes by Artie. He's got a record for assaults, but never more serious than bar fights. Or at least nothing he's been caught for. He's been working for Vinnie for about four years," Phil told her.

"Do you have his Social?"

"Yeah, I wrote it down just in case. Here you go," Phil said.

"Thanks. I'll run this while the program is working on the password."

She opened a file on her desktop and typed in the information.

"There you are! We've got him," she said, turning to the detectives with a big smile on her face.

"He's the one who got the money from Vinnie?" Dennis asked.

"Yeah. They're going to argue it was for something else, but that's for you and the lawyers to figure out."

A ping sounded and Sarah's face brightened.

"Eureka! I knew it would work," she exclaimed. "I've got the password. Now cross your fingers that what we need is on here to tie this up."

She searched through the files on Ted's laptop, taking notes as she found information relevant to Henry's case. She gave the desktop one more scan to make sure she hadn't missed anything.

"Ted had a breakthrough in the investigation, but it was after he'd given the other papers to Dylan Johnson's office to hold for Rachel. You're going to love this," she told them. "But Mike Nicholson is going love it even more."

CHAPTER 47

"That's amazing!" Eva exclaimed when Sarah was finished with her recitation of the events leading up to the discovery of Ted's laptop and the information it revealed.

The sound of a ping on Sarah's phone announcing a text interrupted her follow-up. She held up a finger as she read the message and a big grin spread across her face.

"That was from Phil. They got Vinnie and Arthur O'Donnell. O'Donnell was caught in Massachusetts so they're waiting for the extradition order to go through, but that's coming. He'll be facing charges for Ted's murder. Vinnie's been charged for a bunch of drug charges. He took over Adam Parker's organization and was using the construction business to do his laundering. They were able to get a confession for the murder-for-hire, too, in return for a plea deal that will reduce his prison time. That part I'm not as happy about, but he'll be spending time behind bars. We did it!"

"Mostly you, Sarah. Well done!" Annalise congratulated her.

Jennifer raised her glass of sparkling water. "Raise your glasses, ladies. A toast for Super Sleuth Sarah who has come through once again."

"Hear! Hear!" the others joined in and clinked their glasses.

"This is going to make planning our memory quilt party even more of a celebration," Eva said. "Have you heard back from Vivian and Meghan, Sarah?"

"I did. Would the Saturday after next be enough time for you to finish Rachel's quilt, Jennifer?"

"Absolutely. I'll probably have it done even sooner, but that gives me some breathing space in case there's a family emergency in the meantime."

"Should we invite our partners, too? And the detectives? They've all had a part in this in one way or another," Eva asked.

"That's a great idea. I know Dave is going to be relieved that it's over even though I've kept my promise to him to stay out of this case," Jennifer said.

What about me? Reuben said as he walked into the room and sat in front of Eva's chair.

"Reuben, you live here. It's not like we could exclude you, but of course, you're invited," Eva reassured him. "I'll even get you a special treat. Just this one time, though. Remember what Dr. ..."

I've got it. I've got it. Reuben's a fatty.

"This is not about body shaming, Reuben. It's about your health. Believe it or not, I want you around as long as possible." She patted her lap for him to jump up and then scratched him behind his ears in the spot she knew he loved.

He closed his eyes in rapt contentment and began to purr.

"Any ideas for the menu? Should we try for a hunter theme for the party, too? Or something that's more about memories?" Eva asked.

"You mean like what foods Ted and Lily liked? And Annalise's parents?" Jennifer asked.

Eva looked surprised. "It wasn't a conscious thing, but now that you've said it out loud, that's exactly what I meant. Thanks, Jennifer."

"That's an easy one. Lily loved anything chocolate but her

favorite was double fudge cake. Ashley makes the best one ever. I'll ask her to make it," Sarah said.

"My dad's favorite dish wasn't very fancy. It was your basic pot roast with onions, carrots, and potatoes. Mom loved any kind of bread. Oh, that reminds me, I brought the sourdough starter and recipe for each of you so don't forget to take one home with you," Annalise said. "So, count me in for pot roast and a loaf of bread. I'd better make that two loaves considering how many people we'll have."

"I'll reach out to Rachel to invite her and find out what Ted's favorite dish was," Jennifer said. "That will be my contribution for the food since I'm the one who started all of this. I'll ask Phil and Dennis if they'd like to come, too." She stopped as though something had suddenly occurred to her. "You know, I don't remember if they've ever mentioned their wives, but should we ask?"

The ladies looked toward the others, the same expression that Jennifer had now on their faces.

"I don't remember either, but yes, we should at least invite them and let them decide," Sarah suggested.

Eva and Annalise both nodded their agreement.

"And I'll make a lasagna in case we have any vegetarians," Eva said. "This is going to be one of the most special potlucks we've ever had. I can't wait."

CHAPTER 48

The day of the celebration and presentation of the quilts had finally arrived. Guests were scattered throughout Eva's house and the sounds of conversation and laughter created a festive mood despite the reason for the gathering.

"Eva, thank you for hosting this. The photo collages are wonderful," Rachel told her. They were standing in front of the one for Ted.

"Annalise and I had a great time putting them together. We were lucky to get so many photographs of Ted and Lily, and Annalise's parents, too. We thought it might be hard to find ones that were taken with them wearing the clothes we used to make the quilts, but everyone we asked came through."

"I didn't know Lily or Annalise's parents, obviously, but being able to see their photos really helped me connect with them."

"Have you met Vivian, Lily's sister?"

"Not formally."

"Let me introduce you. She's the one in the red dress and Sarah is the one in navy."

Rachel looked in their direction and focused on Sarah. "Sarah? Isn't she the one who Ted visited?" Rachel asked.

Uh oh. I hope this isn't going to be a problem, Eva thought, but put on a cheery smile. "Yes, she's the one," she replied, and led the way to where Vivian, Meghan, Sarah, and Ashley were gathered around the posterboard with Lily's photos.

"Hello, ladies. I'd like to introduce you to Rachel Hartley, Ted Hartley's widow." Eva made the introductions and held her breath, but was pleasantly surprised when Rachel put her arms around Sarah and hugged her tightly. Sarah's eyes widened as she looked at Eva questioningly.

"I can't thank you enough for what you did to prove that Ted's death wasn't an accident. I can even forgive you for talking to my husband in your bedroom." She released Sarah and had a big grin on her face.

Vivian and Meghan looked at Sarah, their eyebrows raised.

"Not in the flesh," Ashley told them.

"Ashley spent the entire time with her head buried under the comforter," Sarah added which resulted in a side-eye from Ashley and laughter from the others.

"Seriously, though, it was a team effort and I'm just happy that we were able to help," Sarah said.

"The ladies did the same for us. If it wasn't for them, my sister's reputation would have been tarnished forever. But now I know the truth and I can be at peace knowing she is, too," Vivian said to Rachel and gave her a hug in solidarity of their shared experience.

Their conversation was interrupted when Jennifer tapped a spoon on her wine glass to get everyone's attention. When the room had stilled and all eyes were on her, she began.

"Thank you all for coming. It fills my heart with joy to see you all gathered here to commemorate the memories of those we've lost. We're going to first enjoy all this delicious food. Thank you also to everyone who donated for the cause. The four of us who are the heart and soul of the Cozy Quilts Club come together every week for a potluck dinner before we begin our quilting projects. But I think I can speak for all of us when I say that this is the most special one we've ever hosted and it's not just because of the food. It's because of the love, care, and commitment of everyone in this room in whatever role you've played to bring justice to those we've lost and celebrate their lives and memories. Phil and Dennis, we can't thank you enough for believing in us when we've come to you for help. You've always been there for us. Well, maybe not quite as much when you first met us," she teased, grinning at them, and was joined with chuckles from around the room.

The detectives' cheeks both turned a shade of pink remembering their first experiences with the women's paranormal abilities.

"And to our families and friends who've supported us on our adventures." She looked directly at David, who bent his head and shuffled his feet. "We love you all. And now, please raise your glasses in a toast to the ones who are no longer with us. Till we meet again!"

"There's no need to be formal tonight. Fill up your plates and find a seat wherever you like," Eva said once the toast was over. "And no matter how much he begs, please don't feed Reuben. I'll give him a treat later."

She knew he was in the living room but could swear she felt his eyes glaring at her as though he'd heard.

"This is quite the spread you ladies have put together," Jim told Eva as he heaped food onto his plate.

"I'll second that," David Ryder said, as he followed Jim around the kitchen island where the food had been set up buffet style.

"We may have outdone ourselves this time," Eva agreed. "Our potlucks are always tasty but this one is spectacular."

"You do this often?" Phil asked as he took a plate and utensils from the stack on the island.

"Every week for our quilt club meetings. There's a lot more

food this time, but we always have a four-course meal," Eva told him.

"We picked the wrong occupation. We should have been quilters," Dennis said to Phil, waiting for his turn for food.

"You're always welcome, but I think we're happy you chose to be detectives. We might not be having this celebration otherwise," Annalise said.

"Fair point. I don't think quilting was my calling," Phil said.

When dinner and dessert were finished, everyone moved into the living room so the quilts could be presented.

"Why don't you start with yours Jen? It was the inspiration for all of our quilts," Eva suggested.

Jennifer took one of the three boxes placed on a card table in a corner of the room and handed it to Rachel.

"I hope you like it. Annalise helped me with some of it so I've added her name to the label on the back. I'd also like to thank Ted for not being afraid of color. It's a lot more interesting than if he'd only worn white shirts. It was an honor and a privilege to do this for you."

Rachel wiped a tear from the corner of her eye and took the box from Jennifer. She sighed when she took it out of the box and held it up to examine before turning it so that the others could see as well.

"Jennifer—and Annalise--this is just beautiful. When I asked you to make the memory quilt from Ted's shirts, I had an idea in my head of how it might look but this has exceeded my expectations. I will treasure it always. Thank you so much for creating what is truly an heirloom piece that will bring me comfort for many years. I'm so happy I found out about memory quilts before donating his shirts or keeping them in a box gathering dust. Let me give you a hug. And you, too, Annalise."

It took a moment to compose herself before Rachel could continue.

"And to Detectives Roberts and Smith, you will have my eternal gratitude for taking on Ted's case and not letting it slip by as an accident. Knowing that Vinnie Barnes and Arthur O'Donnell will stand trial for his murder has helped bring me closure. Thank you."

The room erupted in applause and once again, the detectives' cheeks turned a rosy shade of pink.

"I told you we should have brought our wives, Dennis. Our reputation might have gone up a notch with them after hearing those words of praise. Seriously, though, it's our job, ma'am, but knowing the peace it's brought to you makes every minute we spent putting together this case in order to arrest them worth it," Phil said.

"Ditto," Dennis said.

"My partner is a man of many words," Phil teased, as the room filled with laughter.

Sarah looked at Eva. "Should I go first?"

"I think that would be the right way to do it," Eva replied.

Sarah took the second box and brought it to Vivian.

"Jennifer has already used all the words so I won't repeat them. But I hope you like how this turned out," Sarah said and was about to walk away when Vivian grabbed her wrist and pulled her back.

"Don't think you're going to leave me here alone," she scolded. She took the cover off the box and placed it on the floor. Her eyes began to water as she ran her fingers over the top of the quilt, soaking in the softness of the fabrics and thinking of the times she'd seen her sister wearing the clothes from which it had been made. "Lily would have loved this." She embraced Sarah in a bear hug.

"Viv, I can't breathe," Sarah gasped.

Vivian loosened her grip and whispered *I love you* into Sarah's ear before releasing her.

"I need to add my thanks to the Cozy Quilts Club ladies and the detectives for vindicating Lily and her reputation. It means everything to me. Just like Rachel, I'm going to treasure this."

"You're up, Eva," Sarah said.

Eva took the last box from the table and presented it to Meghan.

"I had no one to make a quilt for so I was happy to do this for you and Panda, because I'm sure he'll be claiming this, too."

"You know he will," Meghan replied.

"I hope you like it."

Meghan opened the box and took out the quilt for everyone to see.

"It's perfect. Just perfect," she said, her voice almost a whisper. "I recognize all of these clothes." She began to laugh and then pointed to one of the blocks. "Lily and I were having one of our girls nights the last time I remember her wearing this. I'd share the story with you, but Vivian just mentioned how much it meant to have Lily's reputation restored. I wouldn't want to tarnish it all over again."

Laughter erupted around the room.

"Thank you, Eva," she said and gave her a hug. "You'll have to come to visit Panda and me soon so we can have a good chat." She winked discreetly at Eva. Meghan was among those who knew of Eva's ability to talk to animals.

"I would love that."

Annalise rose to address the group and held up the wall hanging she had in her lap.

"I'm not able to give it to them, but this wall hanging was made from clothes my mom and dad wore. They *were* gathering dust in the attic," she said, looking toward Rachel, "so I need to thank you for coming up with the idea for a memory quilt. This is a representation of my house, well, *our* house. The one my parents owned and I grew up in and am living in now. They loved that house, as do I, and I think they would have cherished this."

"It's beautiful, Annalise," Rachel said.

"Thank you, and now back to our regularly scheduled program," Annalise finished.

Applause filled the room and the guests broke off into

smaller groups for conversation. Vivian, Meghan, and Rachel were sitting on the couch together showing off their quilts and sharing stories and laughter about Ted and Lily as different blocks brought back memories.

Annalise and Eva hung back surveying the scene. Annalise tipped her head toward Eva and nodded her chin in Jim and Liam's direction. They were deep in discussion in the far corner of the room facing away from them.

"What do you suppose those two are up to?" Annalise asked.

"There's one way to find out," Eva replied and walked toward the men.

"One thing you're going to figure out—if you haven't already —is that these ladies always seem to be wrapped up in a new adventure. The best way to handle that is to just go with the flow because they're four very strong women and they're going to do what they're going to do regardless of our opinions," Jim was saying.

"Is that so?" Eva said, startling him.

Instead of being apologetic, though, he gave her a kiss on the cheek and grinned broadly at her. "It's the secret to the success of our relationship, don't you agree?" he asked, and winked at Liam. "That's what I was just telling Liam."

"I would have said it's because we don't live together," Eva said, drily.

"Well, there's that, too," Jim agreed.

"What do you think, Annalise?" Liam said, as he moved aside for her to join the group. "Has Jim given me good advice?"

"Not entirely. I'd like to think we keep an open mind and listen to advice. It's just that we like our own advice better— most of the time, but not always."

"So, there's room for discussion, then?" Liam asked.

"Always."

"Sorry to interrupt, but we need to be going and we wanted to thank you for inviting us. The food was amazing and it truly was nice to hear how much it meant to everyone for just doing our jobs," Phil said.

"I'll second that," Dennis agreed.

"Like I said, a man of few words—at least today," Phil teased.

"We're sorry we didn't get to meet your wives, but maybe we can do that in a smaller group sometime," Eva said.

"I hope so. They probably feel like they know you already as much as Phil and I sing your praises," Dennis said.

"Are you leaving?" Jennifer asked as she and Sarah joined the group.

"Yes, but we hope we'll see you again. Maybe the next time we can do it as a purely social event," Dennis suggested pointedly.

"That would be a nice change of pace," Sarah agreed. "Ashley and I need to be heading out, too. Vivian wanted to see Meghan's new apartment and they invited us to come along."

"Don't let them go without saying goodbye to us," Eva said. "Come on ladies, we can leave the men to figure out how they're going to handle us."

"Ouch," Liam said under his breath, but loud enough that Jim heard, eliciting a chuckle.

"That sounded worse than it was. That's also part of the equation for how we get along. We can rib each other, but it's mostly for show."

"Well, ladies, we pulled it off," Eva said, once the other guests had said their goodbyes. They had gathered in the kitchen to put away the leftovers while the men were watching a football game in the living room.

"Are you talking about the party or the case?" Jennifer asked.

"I meant the party, but it does work for both."

"Do you ever wonder if we were brought together for more than just the quilting?" Annalise asked.

"I've thought about that, too, and I believe we were," Jennifer said.

"Me, too," Eva agreed. "But either way, I'm glad we met."

CHAPTER 49

"You're awfully quiet," Jennifer commented, looking over at David from her passenger seat on the ride home from the party.

"I was just thinking about how much you've changed since joining the quilt club."

She cocked her head questioningly, not sure where he was going with this. "Oh?"

He took his eyes off the road to look at her, his expression serious.

"I mean that in a good way. You're really coming into your own. You've always been a great wife and mom, but now you're becoming more confident about yourself, not just an extension of the kids and me."

"Ah," she said, nodding and reflecting on what he said.

"You know I'm proud of you—always. But that speech you gave tonight and the one you gave at Summer's memorial service have shown me a completely different side of you. Sometimes I look at you now and wonder who this generous, compassionate, and confident person is and why I never really saw you in that way until now."

"Mmm hmmm." Jennifer replied. He glanced at her when he felt her frowning at him.

"I'm messing this up, aren't I?" he asked, with a sheepish grin.

"Possibly, but I'm going to give you some slack to explain yourself," she said, keeping her tone light.

He paused a moment, considering his words before continuing.

"I guess what I'm saying is that I admit I had been taking you for granted, but now I'm seeing you with new eyes. And I like what I see and it's made me realize how lucky I am to have you as my life partner and friend."

Her face scrunched up in an aww expression.

"Thank you. That means a lot to me. We're both about to enter a new phase of our life with the kids graduating from high school soon and going off to college. I don't know if I've changed exactly, or if that was just a part of me that was waiting to blossom, but I do feel different since I've been with the quilt club ladies. Partly because of how we've helped so many people who lost loved ones, including us when we lost Aunt Sadie, but also how I think all of us feel valued since we started this whole crime solving adventure."

"But we..." David began.

"I know what you're about to say," Jennifer interrupted. "Yes, you and the kids value me, but this isn't the same. Whether it's wrong or right, I think a lot of us take for granted that the ones closest to us do value us. So, when someone outside that circle appreciates you and acknowledges that you've contributed a skill that helped them and others, and may have even saved lives, it means more." She sighed. "Now I'm the one who's messing this up."

David reached out his hand to take hers and gave it a soft squeeze.

"We're good. I know what you mean."

"So does this mean you'll be okay with it if I'm more involved if we have another case to solve?"

He sighed. "Okay might be stretching it, but what I can say is that I won't stand in your way to do what you have to do to help. And that I'll trust you to make the right decisions to keep yourself safe."

"That's all I can ask. Thank you for understanding how important this is to me."

"It's going to cost you a batch of oatmeal raisin cookies," he teased.

"You've got it," she said, chuckling. "I love you," she said, her voice serious now.

He turned to face her and gave her a wink. "Love you, too."

EPILOGUE

"Another month, another quilt to make," Eva said to the ladies at the next club meeting.

"Another mur…" Sarah began but was quickly interrupted by Jennifer.

"Don't even think what I know you're thinking!"

"I second that!" Eva said. "After our party, I thought a lot about friendship, so of course I had to look up quilt patterns with friendship in the name. I really like this one. It's called Friendship Star and there are several variations of it, but I liked this one the best." She put the printout in the middle of the table so everyone could see.

"This would be a good one for using up fabrics we already have, wouldn't it?" Sarah asked.

"You're absolutely correct," Annalise said, smiling. "How big is your fabric stash these days? You must be catching up to us now."

Sarah laughed. "Not by a long shot, but you all had a few years head start on me. But I'm catching up faster than I thought I would."

"I like this, Eva. The pattern is beautiful and it would always make me think of the four of us. We could use another blanket in the rec room for snuggling up while we're watching TV. The kids are always fighting over the one that's there now."

"That's a perfect sentiment, Jennifer. I love the idea of making a quilt that would commemorate our friendship. Although I think of us as sisters now and I can't imagine my life without all of you in it. We've become so much more than friends and I still have to remind myself every so often that it's been less than a year since the four of us met. You'd already left, Sarah, but after the party we talked about there being a higher purpose for why we found each other," Annalise said.

"Oh, I absolutely believe that," Sarah said, nodding her head vigorously. "I know my life is a whole lot better with the three of you in it. It helped me finally open up to Ashley about being able to communicate with ghosts. Keeping it secret for nearly all of my life was hard. Now I know I've got people who get it because you've all been there, too. Ashley is still adjusting, but she'll get there," she said, grinning.

Eva grabbed her phone at the first ring, apologizing to the others. "I'm so sorry. I thought I'd silenced this. I'll just send it to voice mail." When she looked at the caller ID, her hand hesitated over the screen, and her eyebrows scrunched together. "I should probably take this. I'll be right back."

Their eyes followed Eva as she walked away and then back to each other, their eyebrows raised in a *what was that about* way. She returned several minutes later, a worried expression on her face.

"That was my old friend, Maggie Larkin. I hadn't heard from her for a while. She's an investigative journalist so she's away a lot when she's researching stories."

"Wait. Is that the same Maggie Larkin who broke the story about that corporate corruption case? I think the CEO's name was something like Wayne Harrison," Sarah said.

"Harrington. And, yes, that's her," Eva replied. "She's back in town for a few days and wants to get together. I should have let it go to voice mail, but with Maggie, you never know if she'll call back and I've been thinking about her a lot lately. I guess she picked up on my vibes."

Annalise had remained quiet while the others were talking and Eva noticed that her eyes looked unfocused.

"Annalise, are you alright?" she asked.

"You need to warn her. She's in danger," Annalise replied and then blinked her eyes several times, as though awakening from a dream.

Sarah sighed. "Here we go again."

———

Continue the Series
The story isn't over yet.
Return to Glen Lake and see what the quilt club uncovers next.
Explore the Cozy Quilts Club Mysteries

———

Stay Connected
Join my reader newsletter
Be the first to hear about new releases, special discounts, and exclusive bonus content.
Sign up for the Newsletter at marshadefilippo.com
OR
Get notified automatically when new books release.
Follow me on Amazon
Follow me on BookBub

———

A Quick Favor
Reviews help other readers discover the Cozy Quilts Club mysteries.

If you enjoyed this book, would you consider leaving a short review on Amazon? Even a few sentences make a difference. Thank you for being part of the quilt circle.

———

Has this book inspired you to make your own memory quilt? To help you get started, download your free copy of Pieces of the Past: A Memory Quilt Journal.

Inspired by the Cozy Quilts Club, this is a printable journal with tips and prompts to get your creative juices flowing. It includes sections for

- Memory Block
- In Loving Memory
- Childhood Treasures
- Wedding Memory Quilt with a bonus section of wedding quilt patterns and memory integration ideas
- Quilt of Gratitude
- Keepsake Box Sketch Page

DOWNLOAD YOUR COPY
Pieces of the Past: A Memory Quilt Journal

https://dl.bookfunnel.com/52gpfpypdp

ALSO BY MARSHA DEFILIPPO

Arizona Dreams (The Arizona Series)

Later-in-life romances about second chances, lasting love, and deep emotional connection—with on-page intimacy.

Arizona Dreams (Seasons of the Heart)

Later-in-life romances about second chances and lasting love—told in a clean, closed-door style.

The Destiny Inn series

A gentle magical-realism series set in a timeless inn, where travelers arrive when they need it most and leave forever changed.

A Cozy Quilts Club Mystery series

A cozy mystery series featuring a small-town quilt club whose members use their paranormal gifts to solve murders—one stitch at a time.

The Quilt of Forgotten Secrets

A Cozy Quilts Club Bonus Story. Available as Ebook and Audiobook formats

Read: https://BookHip.com/MCXWBJK

Listen: https://ihave.spoken.press/p/6f6i3VshmzU

www.ingramcontent.com/pod-product-compliance
Lightning Source LLC
Chambersburg PA
CBHW030928060726
47591CB00005B/1708

9781956240221

ABOUT THE AUTHOR

After retiring from her day job of nearly 33 years, Marsha DeFilippo has embarked on a new career of writing books. She is also a quilter and lifelong avid crafter who has yet to try a craft she doesn't like. She spends her winters in Arizona and the remainder of the year in Maine.

For more information, please visit my website:
marsha defilippo.com

To get the latest information on new releases, excerpts and more, be sure to sign up for Marsha's newsletter.
https://marshadefilippo.com/newsletter

facebook.com/Marsha-DeFilippo

instagram.com/marshadefilippo

bookbub.com/authors/marsha-defilippo

pinterest.com/defilippo0699

amazon.com/author/marshadefilippo

marshadefilippowriter.substack.com